I0579986

The Baker of Gippsland

A Trilogy of Supernatural Mysteries

Peter Donelly

The Baker of Gippsland
Peter Donelly

To my parents
Harold Edward Donelly
Edna Edith May Donelly

ISBN: 978-1-7637519-0-3

Copyright © 2024 Peter Donelly

Email: bakerofgippsland@gmail.com

All Rights Reserved.

All rights reserved. No part of this publication may be reproduced, distributed, or transmitted in any form or by any means, including photocopying, recording, or other electronic or mechanical methods, without the prior written permission from the author, except in the case of brief quotation embodied in critical reviews and certain other noncommercial uses permitted by copyright law.

First Printing 2024

Table of Contents

The Baker of Gippsland

Bruthen

1936

It seemed to be the perfect house for the family, but appearances can deceive. An unseen tenant in this place of misery was looking for someone to take away his pain.

"It's a wonderful house, just right for your family; plenty of big airy rooms, a well-equipped kitchen, and enough land for a large vegetable garden," enthused Alan Shears, the Bairnsdale-based real estate agent as he reeled off the features of the rental property.

Bill and Sarah O'Connell and their two young daughters had well and truly outgrown the poky joint they rented on the outskirts of Bruthen. It was hardly ideal; they shared a kitchen with the owners, who made beef and vegetable stew every third day and left it decomposing on the stove in the meantime to be reheated at lunch and dinner. The mice were a problem, but the rats were unbearable.

They needed more space and somewhere close to Bill's work at the local bakery. The doctor's house, as it was known locally because of Doctor Crawford, who'd practised there years ago, had unexpectedly become available after being shut up for many years. Despite being vacant for so long, the house and property had been well maintained, and Bill and Sarah readily agreed to inspect it after the agent unexpectedly contacted them.

The weatherboard and corrugated iron roofed house stood high on solid red gum stumps, larger than most houses in the vicinity yet unobtrusive, set back on the Bruthen hill a couple of hundred yards from the cemetery. Bill and Sarah were surprised by its size: three large bedrooms and a spacious kitchen with a wood stove and preparation area. Sarah sighed deeply when she saw it—blessed freedom from the dirty shared kitchen and hopefully the vermin. It would be perfect for making her preserves and pickles to keep their food costs down and perhaps sell to make some pocket money.

Bill loved the place—certainly far better than any house he'd ever lived in and the asking rent was reasonable. But there were two odd rooms that puzzled him: a front parlour with a pressed metal ceiling and a small adjoining room—a laboratory of some kind containing chemicals and instruments.

"Eh, those two front rooms?" he asked Alan.

Alan diverted himself from checking his fly buttons. "Yes, they're the rooms the doctor used—his surgery and the laboratory," he quickly explained. "I'm told the chemicals are harmless, but best keep it locked up. That's what the owner in Melbourne wants. You can use the surgery for a parlour—well, once you furnish it."

"And who is the owner in Melbourne?" Bill asked.

The agent's face lost its ever-present smile, and his fingers once again started to head south before he checked himself.

"A lady owner who wants to keep her name out of it," he said bluntly. "She probably wouldn't rent the place in normal times, but given the depression we're in, everybody's looking for more income, eh?"

"That makes sense," said Bill. "But I'd like that laboratory cleaned out. Sarah might like to use it for storage, and in any case, the kids might get into the chemicals."

"Yes, alright. I'll check with the owner, but best to keep it locked until I advise otherwise," said Alan.

"If you don't mind, we'll take another walk through the place before we make our decision," Bill said.

"Sure, go ahead, said Alan. "I'll stay here and have a smoke."

Bill and Sarah strolled slowly along the Baltic pine floor in the hallway.

"This will be a beauty to behold when I finish waxing and polishing it," Sarah whispered enthusiastically. "And the cream-painted wainscoting like lines of soldiers standing to attention. I've always wanted to have a wainscoted hallway."

They both loved the bedrooms—clean, large and airy, illuminated by soft light coming through the large, full windows.

Sarah stood in the middle of the kitchen, imagining the aroma of a lamb shank stew and dumplings filling the air as Bill sat playing with the girls around the table. From the back veranda, the scenic view down the rolling hills towards the highway and the wide shallows of the Tambo showed the country at its best.

"It will be wonderful to relax out there on those hot summer evenings," Sarah said contentedly.

Their inspection confirmed what they already knew: this was the place for them. In time, they could get rid of the laboratory and change the parlour into a comfortable front room. They really could make it into a grand family home. As they went to find Alan, Bill heard a noise coming from the laboratory—a small smashing sound. Then, a frigid gust of air surprisingly blew into his face, stopping him in his tracks. He looked at Sarah, but she registered nothing and was only intent on letting Alan know they would take the house. Bill thought nothing more about it, putting it down to the wind in this elevated part of town.

Alan was waiting for them outside, beaming a wide smile. "Well, what's the verdict—take it or leave it?" he challenged.

Bill was about to say they would take it but instead asked about a concern.

"Alan, just how many people have shown an interest in the property or inspected it?"

Alan's smile disappeared again, and for a moment, he looked flustered. "Yes, well, you are the first to show interest, but it hasn't been on the market very long. Arthur Jenkins—he's my boss—he told me you might be interested. You know Arthur from the Masonic lodge in Bairnsdale, don't you?"

"Yes, I know Arthur, but not very well. I'm just wondering why more people aren't showing an interest in such a good property."

Alan looked uncharacteristically serious. "Look, things are fairly quiet at the moment in regard to rental properties—there's just not a lot of money about. You know that. If you want to pass on the property, that's fine. I'm sure I'll find someone else."

It wasn't much of an answer, but in any case, Bill told Alan they would take the property. He couldn't help noticing that Alan sighed with relief before saying he would get the documents finalised as soon as possible so they could take possession in the next few days.

———————

Bill started work around 11 p.m. and finished up when his boss, Hodges, arrived at 7 a.m. to serve in the shop. Hodges had originally been the baker but injured his back moving heavy bags of flour. He'd approached Bill at their Masonic Lodge meeting and offered to teach him baking if he would do the heavy work. That was three years ago, and now Bill did all the baking while Hodges took care of the shop during the day. Working through the night by himself had been a challenge at first because, more than anything, he relished the company of people—familiar or not—and their chatter on all manner of things. But he quickly discovered the contentment of being with his own thoughts, recalling what had happened earlier in his life and planning the future.

Everything had fallen into place nicely. Marrying Sarah and having two healthy girls had changed him from a drifter, a lonely bachelor, to a man with his feet firmly planted on the ground. Then there was the job offer from Hodges, and learning baking and having people appreciate his bread had rounded out his new life. He now felt settled, maybe for the first time in his life. Childhood in the remote bushland shanty town of Deptford had been anything but settled, let alone happy. His father, a gold miner, had been overbearing—a bully. He bullied Bill's mother and his kids as well as anyone who crossed his path. Much of this could be explained by the simple fact that he dug his gold mines in the wrong places—he could find gold, but not enough to cover the expenses of extracting it. It was a similar story with the other miners in town—too little gold to cover operating costs or even their living expenses.

Bill's one consolation in Deptford was the one-room schoolhouse the government had set up for the education of the town's children. Mr Mason was the sole teacher, and apart from taking classes for kids ranging in age from six to fourteen, he tried panning for gold after school hours. He was spectacularly unsuccessful, as Bill's father often reminded him. However, Mr Mason did manage to teach his students to read and write and do simple arithmetic, but in Bill's view, his greatest strength was his daily storytelling, usually about the glories of the British Empire, the battles it had fought and won and all the countries it had conquered.

They were grand tales, and Bill sat spellbound as Mr Mason enthusiastically recounted stories of Lord Nelson, the Duke of Wellington, Edith Cavell, and the East India Company.

It was a lack of gold and the isolation that finally put paid to Deptford. As the people became poorer, desperation set in, and they began to drift away. When Bill's thirteen-year-old brother, Fred, died of twisted bowel, those who remained in town, including his family, said they'd had enough and left the place to the wallabies and encroaching bush.

After some tough years working on the roads and digging spuds, Bill's life had turned out well, contrary to his father's prediction that he would amount to nothing much. Slim and standing nearly six feet tall, the years of hard work had left him strong in the forearms with more than enough stamina to work mounds of dough and shoulder bags of flour without raising a sweat. Fair in complexion and softly spoken, a receding hairline was his only real concession to ageing. He had every reason to be happy, so he could not account for the ominous feeling that had taken hold of him since renting the house. Alan Shears' curious response about the lack of interest in the house was still playing on his mind. Was he hiding something, or was it simply a case of his Masonic friend giving him first crack at a property that suited his family so very well? Perhaps he was reading too much into Alan's reaction.

Bill couldn't help thinking that life was going too well for him these days. Surely, something would happen to bring him back to earth with a thud. That's how he thought; *when life is going well, something is sure to come along and wreck it.*

Settling into the new house took no time. Sarah's parents provided new bedroom furniture and some of their unused chairs they'd stored away. People around town gave them buckets, mops, vases—all manner of odds and ends. Even Bill's father sent him a sugar bag of old tools and a scythe for cutting the grass. Bill remembered him using it and looking like the Grim Reaper often portrayed in the city newspapers.

Sarah had never been happier and was setting up their home just the way she wanted it: neat and orderly and, above all, scrupulously clean. Bill cut the grass into a passable lawn and started digging the vegetable garden, planting potatoes and carrots along with a row of silver beet and beans against a trellis fence. After a couple of weeks, they had themselves a cosy nest, and everyone was content as a new stage in their lives began.

The first incident occurred about a month after moving into the house. Sarah was making good on her daydream of putting up a lamb shank stew and dumplings for the family while Bill and the girls played with a deck of cards at the table. The warm kitchen was suffused with the succulent aroma of the stew, and excited shrieks from the girls gushed forth as Bill taught them how to play Snap with a complimentary lesson in cheating that was far more intriguing than the game itself. A sudden, loud smashing of glass or crockery came from the laboratory that made everyone jump and turn towards the locked room. The kitchen fell silent apart from the gentle bubbling of the stew, and the light-hearted mood in the room evaporated to disquiet and anticipation of another shocking noise.

Bill sat bolt upright, exclaiming, "Shit, what was that?"

Sarah gave him a furious look for swearing in front of the girls, but she was thinking something similar. Bill quickly darted towards the laboratory, expecting to see shattered fragments of some old bottle or flask littering the floor. He slowly unlocked and opened the stiff door, gazing first at the floor, but there was nothing to be seen—everything was in order with no sign of any breakage. But he sensed someone had been in the room and, in some way, could still feel their presence. A slight chill in the air, fading as the seconds passed as if it were disappearing slowly through the walls. And then it was gone, whatever it was.

He stood for a moment surveying the shelves of glassware—phials and gallon jars—which were mostly empty though some had dried white powder encrusted on their insides. God knows what they'd contained, but the dust covering them indicated they hadn't been used for years. Bill recalled the agent telling them to keep the door to the laboratory shut and not to go in there—apparently the owner didn't want it disturbed or anything disposed of. Bill turned around as Sarah pressed against his back, peering over his shoulder, her eyes darting around, trying to see what had fallen to the floor. As she realised nothing was broken, and the floor was not covered with fragments of glass, her face registered amazement, her head shaking slowly at the lack of evidence that should have been abundantly clear. She turned away and went back to the kitchen, not saying a word.

The cold air was the only evidence of whatever had happened in the laboratory. Bill knew someone had been in there, but who or what, he had no idea. He returned to the kitchen and shrugged at Sarah.

"I don't know what happened, but it's all fine," he said, trying to sound confident and adding that there was nothing to worry about. Sarah, who was nursing two scared little girls at the kitchen table, didn't believe a word of what he was saying—the fixed look of concern on her face said it all.

"Bill, what the hell is going on?" she asked, her face strained with worry and incomprehension, her eyes firmly focused on her husband.

"Darling, I really don't know—maybe it's just the wind or some blighter playing a stupid joke," Bill responded slowly and unconvincingly. "I'll have a look under the house tomorrow—there must be some cracks in the floorboards. It'll be alright, you'll see."

Sarah went quiet, clearly shaken by the incident. The family ate their dinner in silence, with everybody expecting another smashing sound, but thankfully it didn't come. At one point, Bill thought he heard the clinking of glass and quickly looked up at Sarah, but she was focused on her food, and that was fair enough because it was delicious.

Bill's mind was racing—there must be some explanation for what had happened. He seized on the Baxter twins, who lived across the road from them. Those twelve-year-olds were always up to no good—dog shit in the neighbours' mailboxes and knocking on people's front doors and running off before they had time to open them. They were carrot-haired, freckle-faced urchins and Sarah detested them on sight saying she would've adopted them out if they'd been hers. Their parents were rough types. Ethel was a huge woman, always wearing a grubby apron. She usually sat on their front veranda as evening fell, her legs splayed wide apart, thankfully covered by a skirt hanging down to her ankles. Bert Baxter, who'd contributed the red hair to his sons, was a large, gruff man who worked at the quarry and propped up the bar at the local hotel for a couple of hours each night before lurching home for supper. He was a good vegetable gardener, though, and kindly left a box of spuds and beans at Bill and Sarah's back door every week or so. But his kids were brats, no doubt about it, and Bill wondered what lark they were up to—maybe they'd found a way to get under the house and were making noises to scare the family. Bill made it his business to keep a close eye on those two and see if there were any signs of them getting under the house.

The new house quickly lost its charm. The family became preoccupied with noises which mainly came from the old laboratory, yet after each occurrence, no evidence of what was causing them could be found. They came to dread sitting down to dinner each night because some strange noise—a smash, a shuffling sound, repeated dull thuds—could almost be guaranteed to occur. Sometimes, it was a low-pitched sound, hardly perceptible but always heard by the now acute hearing of each family member. Bill and Sarah tried to convince themselves and the kids that the sounds came from the settling of the timbers in the house as the cool of night fell. Bill always investigated the smashing sounds in the laboratory, always without results. But he could sense the rising level of anxiety in Sarah and the gaiety and colour leaving his girls' faces. His excuses and theories about the sounds were wearing thin, yet he could not admit that some supernatural force might be at work. If that thought ever arose, he quickly slapped it down and was even angry at himself for thinking that way.

The dreams started around this time, not so much for Bill, but Sarah and the girls were deluged with terrifying visions, mostly in the early morning just before Bill arrived home. The dreams were always the same: a white doctor's coat would appear in the distance, moving forward as if following the actions of an invisible wearer. Slowly, it would come towards the dreamer and in the last few steps, it would billow out and throw itself forward like it was intent on enveloping and suffocating them. Sarah and the girls woke terrified with racing hearts, finding their white bedsheet wrapped around their heads and struggling desperately to get it off before being able to take deep, calming breaths as the awareness they had been dreaming came upon them as a sudden shock.

Bill had a few dreams about the white coat, but not in the same terrifying way as his family. It was as if the coat was trying to lure him towards it and take him somewhere. And in his dreams, there was always a playing card—a two of diamonds—in the breast pocket of the coat. No one in the family mentioned the two of diamonds when they talked about their dreams, and Bill decided to keep it to himself, not wanting to worry his family with what was probably an irrelevant detail.

Bill usually arrived home around 7 a.m. after his night's baking to find Sarah and the girls sleeping soundly together in the big bed. The girls would start the night in their own beds but soon sought the reassuring warmth of Sarah when she turned in. It put paid to Bill's practice of slipping into bed with Sarah shortly after arriving home for a cuddle or better. Anyway, he was content his family was safe and secure together, even if his intimate desires were thwarted. Sarah and the girls would stir on his arrival home and sleepily straggle out to the kitchen, where Bill stirred the black iron stove back to life to make tea and breakfast. With cups of tea and glasses of milk before them, along with toast and apricot jam, the stories of their night emerged: the knocks from the laboratory, the dreams, the sudden waking in a cold sweat before drifting back to an uneasy sleep. The dark circles around their eyes were becoming more prominent by the day, and Bill's exasperation and feeling of helplessness increased accordingly. But breakfast always lifted their spirits, and after their morning wash, Sarah would get the girls dressed for a walk down to the river or some shopping at the general store. Bill would glance over the newspaper he'd brought home with him before heading off to bed before arising around 4 p.m.

This particular morning, the promise of a clear, warm day had inspired Sarah to make some sandwiches and a thermos of tea and take the girls to the sandy part of the river flats where they could safely paddle in the crystal-clear water and chase the ducks that were feeding nearby. Sarah took a few magazines her mother had sent her and the Forges department store catalogue to find some clothes she could mail order at a reasonable price. Bill watched them leave through the front gate, wearing their bonnets and each carrying a bag of food or towels. He was sad not to be joining them but was dog-tired—the lot of every country baker working through the night. He was soon in bed, and sleep came when his head hit the pillow. But only an hour or so later, crashing noises roused him, louder than he'd ever heard before coming as usual from the laboratory.

Tired and exasperated, Bill fumbled his way out of bed, somehow finding his slippers and dressing gown, and dragged his sore frame to the laboratory for what he expected to be another wild-goose chase. He reached for the brass doorknob and withdrew his hand as soon as he touched it. It was frigid, painful to the touch, and he stared at it, expecting to see a crust of ice. But there was none, so he grabbed the knob by insulating his hand with his dressing gown. The knob turned with some effort and the door opened slowly—a puff of freezing air tumbling on him as he entered. The crispness of the air tingled his face and lips, and he wrapped his dressing gown tighter. The room felt enlivened as if he'd walked in on a game of musical chairs where the music had stopped and a cast of characters were standing still, invisible and mute, waiting and looking at him. Bill's eyes cleared and he glanced around the room, trying to catch sight of anyone or anything that might be out of place or unusual, but there was nothing unusual. He walked slowly to the benches and checked the bottles and vials. Some seemed to have moved ever so slightly because there were crescents of clean areas on the bench next to dusty outlines.

The room was gradually becoming warmer, and the charge in the air began to dissipate, but he knew he had been summoned to see or maybe hear something, yet nothing was apparent. As he turned to look at the bench behind him, he caught sight of some marks and quickly focused on them: two diamonds, like on a playing card, had been etched in the dust. Moving quickly to get a closer view, an almost imperceptible draught of air arose, which quickly obscured the marks. He spun around to see if he could spot where the draught had come from, but the room was sealed; no doors or windows open, and the walls were solid without cracks of any kind. The room was still now and had lost its chill. He stood there uncomprehending as to what had happened, even wondering if he had dreamt it all and was sleepwalking. In his heart, he knew this was no dream—something was trying to get his attention and deliver a message. But that message was beyond him, and in its stead, a fearful confusion enveloped him: mind and soul.

He returned to bed, weary and weak, and tried to think things over, but he soon fell into a shallow, disturbed sleep. There was his father, smiling a toothy grin as he swished the scythe in a wide arc from side to side, swearing at each stroke, making no progress, and his swearing becoming worse with each swing. Bill woke with a jolt and realised it was early afternoon; Sarah and the kids would soon return. There would be no more sleep today, and in anguish, he rose to wash. As he looked at himself in the mirror, he thought he might be going crazy.

Bill decided not to tell Sarah about what had just happened—it would only upset her, and in any case, he was certain the message was meant for him alone.

When Sarah and the kids did return, they were rowdy, and their faces were flushed from a day of rollicking by the river. Bill put on a brave face and joined in the fun, wanting to hear everything about their day and teasing the girls about how they could not possibly have paddled up to their knees, with the girls screaming at him that they really did. Sarah, too, had a warmth in her face that had been missing in recent times.

It marked the beginning of a lull in the noises and the terrifying dreams for all of them. Somehow, the house itself felt calm, and the light was warm and even. Sure, they all expected noises, but nothing out of the ordinary occurred, and their dreams were about running through the paddocks of long grass and splashing in the river. Life at home was relaxed, and Sarah busied herself more than ever with sewing clothes, making preserves, and visiting neighbours who were more than up for a good gossip. Sarah's scones were becoming increasingly more famous by the day, and she had a steady stream of admirers asking for her recipe. Bill loved the card nights at their place, with loads of laughs and a chance to think about something other than the laboratory and the noises. Not for a minute did he believe it was over, but he was happy for the respite for everyone's sake.

An uneventful month and a half went by, and the family settled into a cosy routine—the life they had imagined for themselves when they moved into the house. As Bill walked up the hill on his way home from a night's baking, he felt tired yet light-hearted and content. Hopefully, the kids were still asleep, and he could quietly cuddle up to Sarah. It always amused him in the bakery around 5 a.m., just before sunrise, he would feel that familiar stirring in his loins. If he brushed against the workbench, a tingle went around this groin, and he had to take a deep breath and refocus on his baking. Anyway, this morning, Sarah willing, he fully intended to let nature proceed as it wished without discouragement.

He quietly entered the back door, not wanting to wake anyone, but stopped dead in his tracks when he saw Sarah and the kids wrapped in blankets sitting in silence around the kitchen table. The room was bitterly cold and dim. The wood stove radiated no heat at all; if anything, it seemed to be absorbing any heat on offer. Sarah was slumped, head down, with her arms cuddled around herself, trying to get warm or maybe seek reassurance. The girls' pink dressing gowns poked out through the blankets, and they were white-faced, their small hands trembling as they played clumsily with a deck of cards.

"Thank God you're finally home," Sarah sighed deeply as Bill appeared in the room. "We've had a dreadful night; we haven't slept a wink. Those noises from the doctor's rooms kept us up all night. It sounded like a damned brass band playing in there."

Sarah slumped down on the table, again burying her head in her hands, and Bill rubbed her shoulders to comfort her.

Sarah raised herself and pleaded. "Bill, you have to do something to make the noises stop," she said. "Or we just have to get out of here and go someplace else."

The girls sat silently, hand in hand, as if they were in shock. They'd stopped playing with the cards, and tears came to their tired eyes as they saw their mother so upset.

"Alright, tell me what happened last night," Bill quietly asked his wife while he continued to rub her shoulders.

Sarah took a deep breath and let it all out. "Everything was fine after you left for work, and I let the girls stay up to around nine o'clock before putting them to bed. They went off to sleep in no time, and I was exhausted and soon in bed and asleep, too. For some reason, I woke up around two thirty and switched on the lamp to look at the clock, but the air in the room hit me at once. It was like an ice chest, and I had to duck under the blankets to get warm. Bill, I swear, it felt like someone was in the bedroom. Honestly, I thought you'd come home early for some reason. My only thought was to see if the girls were safe, so I jumped up and ran to the door. I've never felt cold like it; it chilled me to the bone, and I thought … I thought I brushed against someone at the end of the bed. My hand froze when I touched the doorknob; it was like a piece of ice.

"The girls were waking up from nightmares when I reached them, and I pulled all the blankets off their beds and carried everything to the kitchen to get away from whatever it was in our bedroom. The kitchen was cold but not frigid, and I tried to get the stove going, but there was no kindling, and I wasn't going outside in the dark for the life of me. God, Bill, what the hell is going on here?"

Bill gathered up Sarah and the girls in his arms and hugged them tight. "Everything is alright now," he reassured them with a firm tone. "Let's get warm and put some grub on the table," he joked as he tickled the girls, which finally brought weak smiles to their faces. He set to work and got the stove blazing hot and soon had a breakfast of hot tea and cocoa and toast with apricot jam on the table. The sun was now flooding the kitchen with bright yellow light, and with the warmth radiating from the stove, the frightening events of the previous evening paled somewhat in the comfort of the family close together, enjoying a simple hearty meal. Sarah was doing her best to throw off the terrors of the night, but in her heart, she knew her family had no future in this house. She would let Bill know in due course that she and the girls would not stay there, not for anything. Tiredness revealed itself soon after, with Sarah and the girls yawning and rubbing their eyes, so Bill packed them off to bed and thankfully heard their soft snoring as quietness once again descended on the house.

He slumped down at the kitchen table before comforting himself with his favourite treat: dripping left over from the Sunday roast spread thickly on bread, well salted. But it had lost its creamy savoury taste as his mind raced over the mountain of problems he faced. Sarah and the girls could take no more; that much was clear. But there was no other accommodation in Bruthen, so his family couldn't just up and move. Maybe it was time for them to take a holiday with Sarah's parents in Mansfield, but that would mean he would be alone, and he dreaded that as much as anything. Still, bringing peace and safety to his family was all that mattered, so if it was time apart, so be it. But gnawing away in the deepest recess of his mind was the growing realisation of what he feared most: whatever it was that was present in this house and causing all the disruption wanted him all to itself. Why, he did not know, but he sensed the terror would only end when he faced up to the presence by himself to find out what it wanted of him. Yet, just as quickly as he considered this idea, he dismissed it. He thought he must be going mad to entertain such rot about spirits trying to communicate with him. Sheer nonsense brought about by a lack of sleep, most likely. Be that as it may, Sarah and the girls had to leave this house, probably forever, and that was the only matter he had to deal with right now.

That afternoon, everyone gathered around the kitchen table to hear Bill's plan. He had checked with Mrs Erskine, his old landlady in town, about whether she had room for Sarah and the girls. He had spun a yarn about Sarah and the girls being a little nervous at night in the house and hearing wild dogs. They just needed a short break to steady themselves. Mrs Erskine wasn't buying Bill's story but said that she could put them up for a couple of days, but then an alternative would have to be found. Bill said that was all the time he needed. The next part of Bill's plan had Sarah and the girls heading off to stay with Sarah's parents in Mansfield for a few weeks while Bill stayed at work and tried to find another place for them in Bruthen. It wasn't much of a plan, but at least Sarah and the kids didn't have to spend another night in the doctor's house. Sarah and the girls greeted it with enthusiasm and relief—the colour came back to their faces as they talked excitedly about Grandma and Pa and their huge woodcutter uncles. They would miss their husband and dad, but at least they would be safe in Mansfield from the terrifying noises and presences.

Sarah went down to the post office to phone her parents, and they were overjoyed to hear of the visit, even if they wondered about the suddenness of it all. Bill bought rail tickets for the next day; that would give them enough time to pack and prepare for the journey. Late that afternoon, as Bill took a nap, a disheartened Sarah packed the cases with enough clothes to last for months. She knew it wouldn't be that long, but she just kept packing anyway. The doctor's house that promised to be a new start for the family, had quickly become a nightmare; Sarah wanted to get herself and the girls as far away from it as possible. But they would be separated from Bill, and that would be hard. Sarah couldn't help but wonder why he intended to keep living at the house after they had left, but he was adamant it would be alright.

Mrs Erskine had prepared a small room with a narrow three-quarter bed and canvas stretchers for the girls—comfortable enough. Bill and Sarah lugged the suitcases down the hill road in the early evening before Bill started work at the bakery, and Sarah and the girls settled into their new room, somewhat downcast but relieved they didn't have to spend another night in the wretched doctor's house.

The next day, after the confusion of getting everyone organised and to the station on time, Sarah and the girls hugged and kissed Bill and tearily but, with relief, boarded the train. Bill, ashen-faced and feeling sick to his stomach, watched as the train slowly pulled out and disappeared around a long curve into the distance. Now it was down to him to find a solution to his family's problem and in quick time. But he didn't have the faintest idea of what to do.

Kneading dough one night soon after the family left, Bill heard the latch open on the side gate of the bakery's fence and turned from his workbench to see his brother Joe stiffly enter the back door along with a blast of cold air. Joe warmed himself by the oven, then slid into a chair at the table to look at the newspaper. Joe was the firstborn son in the family, seven years senior to Bill, and had received harsh treatment from their father, who made him work unmercifully hard in the dusty and cramped confines of the gold mine at Mount Welcome. Joe finally escaped by joining the army as a sixteen-year-old and going to the war in France. The Joe who returned was a steeled and serious man; his father wisely kept his distance but, more importantly, kept his mouth shut when Joe was around. Joe and Bill had been close as kids and remained so as men. By themselves, they said little, content in each other's company.

But now Bill's worries were overwhelming him, and he couldn't hold back.

"Listen, something strange is going on up at the house, and that's why Sarah and the kids are taking a holiday," he blurted out as a kind of exasperated confession.

Joe looked up, feigning surprise. "What are you saying?" he said. "Something strange is going on? Are you telling me the joint is haunted or something?"

Bill quickly tried to head him off, saying he wasn't sure what was happening, but it seemed something unnatural or at least inexplicable was going on.

"Old Doc Crawford's place is haunted," Joe scoffed. "Now I've heard everything."

Bill knew he'd react this way. Joe was a practical man like no other—every problem had a practical solution. For him, nothing out of the ordinary occurred anywhere in the world. He loved tinkering with motors, and to his mind, the entire universe worked like a big machine—predictable and intelligible—if you took the time to look at it closely and make the proper adjustments.

"All the same, noises are happening that just can't be explained. I don't know; maybe some unseen presence is at work?" Bill tentatively suggested, embarrassed he was even talking like this.

"Be buggered," snorted Joe. "No such thing as bloody unseen presences. Those noises will all be down to something natural, most probably the wind," he said while looking at his brother as if he'd gone loopy. "Have you ever thought it might be those little pricks across the street—the Baxters, eh?"

"Yes, yes, thought of that, but it's not them," Bill spat. He decided to shut up. It was no use talking to Joe about such matters, so he made them a cup of tea.

Joe realised he'd been hard and relented. "Listen, I'll get some timber palings and cover up any cracks or holes I find—that'll fix things," he advised, assuring himself more than Bill.

Noticing the worried look on Bill's face, he changed the subject and started talking about the doctor who had occupied the house years earlier.

"Doc Crawford looked after me for a while when I came home from the war. I got some gas in the trenches—not bad, but enough to affect my nasal passages—you know how I snort and sniff. He was a good doctor and tried his best. I once took him shooting and exploring out near our old man's Mount Welcome mine. Then, all of a sudden, he left town and headed for the city. Guess the money he'd make there would have been better than the slim pickings hereabouts."

Joe rose to head off home but cautioned Bill about thinking spooks or any such things were behind the problem. "The old doctor's house is well-built; maybe needs some minor repair, but that's all," he advised. And for good measure, he told Bill to stop paying attention to the hysterical talk of Sarah, who he reasoned was most likely exaggerating the whole situation. Joe started to say that Sarah was missing Bill during the night, but didn't take it too far—he'd made his point.

Bill appreciated Joe's advice, but in his heart, he knew no amount of boards and nails or practical measures would provide the answer. Something else was at work, outside his understanding and that of the people hereabouts. Of course, he'd heard talk of ghosts, but regarded it all as far-fetched stories. Yet here he was, in the midst of some supernatural experience, or so it seemed. He couldn't see a natural cause for what was happening, but the idea of some unseen presence trying to exert its power was…unthinkable. He was at a total loss and just wanted to bring his family back to a safe home.

The next night, the side gate latch again opened, and Bill, expecting another visit from Joe, was surprised when a small, elderly Catholic priest came in through the back door. Puzzled, he stopped work as the priest introduced himself.

"Good evening, Mr O'Connell. I am Father Doolan from St Mary's in Bairnsdale. I've been performing pastoral duties in the area, lodging overnight with the Doherty family," the priest explained with a strong Irish accent. "I couldn't sleep, so I came out for a walk and noticed the lights on in the bakery, and, well, thought I might say hello."

Bill's family was fiercely Protestant, deeply suspicious of Catholics, as were his Masonic friends, but he sensed the priest was a good man. More importantly, it immediately struck him for some reason that this priest was someone who could help him with his problem.

"Come in and warm yourself, Father," the baker said. He made tea and even put up a freshly baked cinnamon bun as the priest sat happily chatting away about the weather and the cool night air playing havoc with his rheumatism.

The priest was fulsome in his praise of the bun. "The last time I tasted cinnamon that good was in India when I was in Cochin," he recalled, screwing up his face.

Bill knew India was part of the Empire, but Cochin was not a place he'd heard of. Anyway, they sat in silence for a time before the baker tentatively tested the priest about strange noises and dreams "… just for the sake of discussion," he said.

"What do you reckon, Father? Is there such a thing as a spirit that can make noises in a house and bring on nightmares, or is that all rot?"

The priest stared fixedly at the baker, not for an instant believing he was initiating a speculative discussion. "You look fraught with worry, man—I noticed it the moment I came into the bakery. Why don't you tell me about the real problem? I'll do all in my power to help."

Bill hesitatingly explained the whole story and even said his brother Joe was boarding up all the holes in the house to stop draughts.

The little Irishman listened closely to the tale, and when it was finished, he sat mulling it over for a minute or two.

"The universe is indeed a mystery," he said. "Sometimes frightening events like lightning can be explained by science, but as for others, there is no obvious or known cause, yet they still occur. During my time in India, the Hindus and Buddhists gave me a new understanding of the universe and how it operates, and while my faith in God is still strong, I can see the strange events you are experiencing are natural, in a sense, but hard to accept because our European minds are no longer open to understanding them."

Then the priest paused, mumbling to himself, and slowly nodded his head before he looked the baker in the eyes.

"Someone from the other side, someone who once lived but has died and is now stuck in some hellish place, is desperately trying to get a message heard by someone, probably to have some action performed here on Earth to correct a past wrong so they can move on to another existence," he said slowly.

The baker was taken aback hearing a Christian man talking like this, but he couldn't help but keep listening, and in his heart, he knew the priest's words made sense in some way or another.

"You have to dispense with your fear and open your heart and mind to true understanding—not to practical solutions but to faith and intuition—to discover some meaning in the signs you are most surely receiving from this troubled spirit. Believe me, all will become clear if you just open yourself—heart and mind. Rest assured, I'll pray for you, Mr O'Connell, but only you can solve this problem."

Then, promising to return soon, the priest stood up and quietly left.

The baker was deep in thought when Hodges arrived to open the shop for the morning trade. Now, at least he had something to go on— find meaning in the messages—and he knew the two of diamonds was the key. Bidding Hodges "Good day" and heading home, the baker almost bumped into a man mounted on a horse directly outside the bakery shop door: Frank Davis, a reclusive local bushman and erstwhile gold panner. Davis was well-known for his staggeringly bad body odour, a smell so overpowering that most people spoke to him at a distance and only for a short period of time. A story was told about one of the local farmers who kept polecat-ferrets he used for trapping rabbits in a small shed. The shed stunk to high heaven, and some of the blokes started betting on who could stay inside the longest.

One after another, they tried, but nobody could stand the stench for more than a minute or so. Then Davis rode up, found out what was going on, and took up the bet. He strode into the shed, and after about thirty seconds, the ferrets ran out!

Bill moved backwards a yard or two while Davis shouted his order for a couple of loaves of bread to Hodges in the shop.

Davis did some gold prospecting but found little. He knew that Bill had once lived in Deptford and asked him about the likely gold mining areas where his father had prospected.

"My father's living down near Koo Wee Rup; certainly not enjoying the high life in Melbourne on the proceeds of his gold mining ventures," Bill explained. "Deptford and Mount Welcome are like most of East Gippsland: there's gold all right, but it's too costly to extract. There might be some alluvial gold after a flood comes down the Nicholson, but don't count on it."

The old bushman sat on his horse, considering the baker's advice. Hodges appeared hurriedly from the bakery door with two wrapped loaves, his face becoming redder as he held his breath and, through gritted teeth, asked Davis how he was going, gave him his bread, thanked him for giving the correct change, and disappeared rapidly back into the bakery. Davis packed his bread and started to ride off. The baker bid him "Good day" and offhandedly said he hoped he'd enjoy the loaves as much as finding diamonds. Davis quickly pulled his horse and turned around to face the baker, a menacing glare in his eyes. "Why did you say a damn fool thing like that, and what have diamonds got to do with anything?"

"I meant no harm, just joking," Bill said.

Davis was agitated and disbelieving but held his tongue while continuing to stare hard at the baker. Eventually, he rode off, giving a quick backward glance at the baker who stood watching the bushman depart, struck by the sudden reaction to what he'd said. And what had he said? He wasn't sure, but it certainly had an effect.

On his way home, he spotted Mrs Erskine picking flowers in her front garden. She ran the boarding house where Sarah and the girls had stayed the night before heading to Mansfield. As the sign outside said, it was a boarding house for gentlemen and spinsters of sober habits. Bill had boarded with her before he married Sarah. Mrs Erskine was a proper lady—elegant and always dressed in florals. Her husband, Edgar, had been station master at Bairnsdale but retired early on account of a bad back, like Hodges. Now, his time was occupied performing odd jobs at his wife's direction, which he complained about on his occasional visits to the local pub, but he made sure he only had the one glass of beer and was home in time for dinner. They'd not had children, so Mrs Erskine's attention was focused on her boarders, and the baker had been one of her favourites. She admired his quiet ways and good manners, and the fact he abstained from alcohol confirmed his worth. But she kept a close eye on him and the other male boarders when refined young women from Melbourne spent their summer holidays at the boarding house. Mrs Erskine would host weekly dinners followed by a musical soiree where she would operate the pianola and lead the singing of songs of the Empire. And sometimes, she would get Edgar to read a poem or two by

Wordsworth or Kipling, something that portrayed the verdant fields of England or tales of exotic India. And all the time, she manoeuvred herself between the young men and women to ensure they weren't getting too close. The evenings would end with a patriotic toast to the King, always performed with cordial served in her best glassware. But as the baker tossed and turned in his bed afterwards, his body and mind enlivened by memories of the shapely figures and perfumes of the city girls, he would hear the low moans of Mrs Erskine and concede that Edgar was still well able to pleasure his wife. Years afterwards, he told Sarah about these nights and that given the chance, he could have pleasured all those city girls in the one night. Sarah scoffed that he was a boaster.

When Mrs Erskine saw the baker, she quickly stopped work. "How are you faring, Bill, without Sarah and girls?" she enquired, insisting that he come for dinner one evening. She would put up his favourite meal: a mixed grill. The baker suddenly realised Mrs Erskine might be able to help him. She was one for the doctors and always running to them with one ailment or another.

"Yes, I'm managing alright so far, Mrs Erskine," Bill replied. "One of your mixed grills sounds like heaven. But I was just wondering if you could help me with something. What do you know about Doctor Crawford, who used to live at my house, just out of interest?"

Mrs Erskine's face tightened. She certainly remembered the doctor and gave Bill a full account of her treatment. When she presented with a bad cold, he had injected some brightly coloured fluid into her, telling her it was a new treatment. But she started to feel worse and was bedridden: delirious and with dreadful pains in her joints. The doctor came calling to check on her after a couple of days, but she wouldn't see him and told Edgar to send him away. She gradually recovered but never again set foot in Doctor Crawford's surgery. Thankfully, he and his family, an odd family, according to Mrs Erskine, not country people, left town some time after.

But ever curious, Mrs Erskine asked the baker about his interest in the doctor. Of course, she had heard tales of strange sounds at the house from Edgar, who earned a few shillings years ago keeping the garden in order, but she put it down to him telling yarns in the pub for attention and a drink on the house. Mrs Erskine wondered if Sarah and the girls had been scared by something in the house. Everyone in town knew something about it but kept it to themselves. Bill was surprised she knew his family's secret but grudgingly accepted you can't keep anything quiet in a place like Bruthen. He mumbled, "My family just needs to spend time with Sarah's folks, that's all, and the wind is the likely culprit for the noises that were disturbing them. Anyway, my brother Joe is going to fix that problem by mending the weatherboards."

Mrs Erskine smiled when he mentioned Joe and asked after him, but the baker, well aware of his brother's reputation when it came to women, quickly closed down the conversation and, looking at his watch, said it was time for him to be off home. Mrs Erskine knew the baker had not given her the whole story, and as she watched him depart, she felt deeply concerned about him and his family. And she felt a twinge of guilt—she had not told the baker everything she knew about Doctor Crawford and his family.

Bill flopped down at the kitchen table after lighting the stove to boil water for tea and a wash. A breakfast of bread and dripping cheered him somewhat, but tired and mentally drained, he went over the events of the night and morning: the priest, Frank Davis, and Mrs Erskine. They were all trying to tell him something, but what? He felt no closer to understanding the riddle that had turned his life upside down. Then suddenly, a noise started coming from the laboratory. He was resigned to them by now and intended to stay put, but then there was an enormous crash and the smashing of glass. Surely, there must be some evidence of it—glass on the floor, whatever. But when he checked, there was nothing—only the dusty benches and old phials in the very same places they'd been the last time he'd checked. The room was not freezing cold this time, and he sensed no presence. But, when he moved closer to the bench, he again noticed something in the dust—some lightly scrawled marks. They looked like two diamonds, but then a draught came from nowhere and blew them away. It all happened in an instant, and he thought his imagination was playing tricks, yet he knew that someone or something he didn't understand was trying to communicate with him.

He retreated to the kitchen, more confused than ever and tired in his body and mind, so after washing his face and hands, he headed to bed, hopefully to find deep and undisturbed rest.

In his restless sleep, the white coat again appeared: motionless, hazy, and transparent at first. Then it slowly moved towards him, and the form of a man took shape—first the head, then the arms and body appeared. The figure was unclear, yet somehow familiar in profile—a strong chin, a haughty expression—it was the image of his father! And then the playing card appeared—the two of diamonds. The baker jolted awake, sweating profusely, heart racing, fearing that the presence in his dream was now inhabiting the bedroom. But his tired eyes saw nothing unusual as he slowly sat up with full consciousness returning. He had slept for ten hours, and it was already late afternoon. He hauled himself into the kitchen and splashed cold water on his face at the sink, then sat at the table. He felt like he'd become a slave to his dreams and fantasies, and maybe he would lose his family because of all this nonsense. It occurred to him that he himself might be responsible for creating these strange events through some unknown power of the mind. Maybe he had infected his family with his bizarre thoughts, projected them somehow, and now he was destroying himself with illusions that seemed real but which he knew were baseless. He wished he had the courage and the pragmatic character of his brother, Joe—as if believing in a world where there is a simple, practical solution to every problem would dispel the misery he was now experiencing. In low spirits, he set about rekindling the fire in the stove and cooked some mutton chops and vegetables. But his appetite was gone, his patience exhausted, and he jumped at the merest noise. He sat there feeling hopelessly defeated and powerless as his meal went cold.

Hodges was carefully stretching his back, his face contorted in mock agony, when Mrs Erskine came into the bakery shop early next morning. Bidding her good morning, he again reminded her of his bad back, casting for sympathy. But Mrs Erskine curtly suggested a good kick up the arse might prove a useful remedy. Hodges protested the use of such language in the shop, which Mrs Erskine rebutted, saying that the dirty yarns he told his cronies every evening at the back of the bakery made her language seem genteel. Anyway, she had no time to talk to him; she wanted to see Bill.

Hodges quickly retreated into the bakehouse and whispered to the baker that Lady Muck demanded his presence in the shop. The baker smiled as he saw Mrs Erskine, and she asked to see him outside, well out of earshot of the nosy Hodges. She lowered her voice and, in soft tones, said, "I didn't tell you yesterday all I knew about Doctor Crawford." Fumbling in her bag, she produced an envelope and said it contained a newspaper clipping from years earlier that had been sent to her by a cousin who lived in Melbourne. "There's something going on in that house of yours, but I don't want to know about it," she whispered. "Such things are best left alone. But I am worried about you and your family, and I think somehow the clipping might mean something and, hopefully, help with whatever it is you're going through." She became emotional, tears welled in her eyes, and excusing herself, she walked briskly across the street towards home.

When the baker arrived home, he read the article from a Melbourne local newspaper, *The Prahran Telegraph*. A handwritten date "1925" was scrawled on it. The headline read, "Death of Local Doctor and Family in Tragic Circumstances." It said that Doctor Crawford, his wife, and eldest daughter had been found dead in their home in Ivy Street, Prahran, as a result of some unidentified poison that had been administered by injection, apparently by the doctor himself. The youngest daughter had survived but was seriously ill in hospital. Police were treating it as a case of accidental poisoning, with the deceased doctor known to be suffering a nervous disease, being held responsible.

The baker leaned back in his chair, slowly shaking his head. He immediately thought about Mrs Erskine and her experience of the doctor injecting her. The man must have been a lunatic to do that to his family. But now, it became crystal clear to the baker that somehow this doctor and his strange ways were at the heart of the mystery confronting him. But what the doctor had to do with the mystery—that was anyone's guess.

Soon after midnight, the baker received the visitor he so eagerly anticipated—the priest. This time, the priest made the tea while the baker finished some high tin loaves. The priest seemed to be expecting some news from the baker, who quickly told him about the talk he'd had with Mrs Erskine and the newspaper article. And he mentioned the strange incident with Frank Davis and the diamonds.

"I am sure the doctor is somehow behind all of this, but how and why, I don't know," he said.

The priest listened without interrupting. Then, staring down at the table, he nodded his head slowly before staring straight into the baker's eyes.

"I, too, consider the doctor the source of the problem—an unstable man, possibly insane," the priest mused. "And such a tragedy to befall his family."

The priest wondered out loud how those events of years ago related to the present-day happenings. If the doctor was apt to haunt a place, surely it would be his old house in Prahran.

"I doubt the doctor is haunting the place. That's a bit far-fetched," said the baker.

But the priest quieted him and said he must be open, heart and mind, to the unseen and unknown if this problem was to be properly dealt with. The baker felt as if he was being tugged in different directions by his practical side, which paid attention to his senses and reasoning, and his other side, intuitive and somehow outside normal reasoning. In any case, he kept listening to the priest.

The priest sensed the baker's dilemma and said, "You have to trust your heartfelt senses and what they were telling you. And more to the point, this problem won't be solved by you staying in the bakehouse. What you need is more information, and it's needed right now. Everything points to the doctor and finding out more about him."

The priest recalled from the newspaper article that the doctor's youngest daughter had not died in the tragedy. Maybe she had survived and was still alive. The baker sprang to his feet and grabbed a copy of the *Sands and McDougall* postal directory Hodges kept in the shop. He checked the entry for Ivy Street, Prahran, and was stunned to read "Miss Alice Crawford, 12 Ivy St." She was listed as the sole occupant of the house—surely, she was the doctor's daughter.

The priest rose to leave and told the baker somehow or other he must go and see this Alice Crawford and find out as much as possible about the doctor.

"I can't just up and leave the bakery," the baker protested. But the priest insisted the next piece of the puzzle would be found with Miss Crawford. The baker knew he was right—he had to go to Melbourne and find out more about the doctor from his daughter. But his first job was to work out a plausible story to tell Hodges to get some time off work.

After arriving in Melbourne with a two-day leave pass grudgingly given by Hodges, the baker sat on the hard wood seat of the Prahran tram, reading the street signs along High Street, looking for his stop. The conductor of the tram had been watching him for some time.

"Where are you heading, cobber?" the conductor asked in a loud, friendly voice.

"Ivy Street, mate. I'm looking to visit a Miss Crawford."

The conductor fixed him with his eyes and moved closer, talking now in hushed tones. He said he knew the story of Miss Crawford well—the daughter of the doctor who'd killed his family, all except her.

"Miss Crawford often used to catch this tram into the city, but not lately. Apparently, she is rather ill," the conductor said as he craned his neck to look out the tram window.

"Ivy Street is the next stop," he said and pulled the cord to alert the driver to stop. He pointed out the street to the baker, who thanked him and eased himself down the steps of the tram.

He wandered up Ivy Street, crossing to the side with even numbers, and came to number 12—a small, tidy Victorian brick house. It had a lush front garden of lilac and pink hydrangeas, and tending to some roses was a woman around his own age. Her slight build and the pale white skin of her arms betrayed a sense of frailty and, as the tram conductor suggested, illness.

He cleared his throat and said, "Good morning. I am hoping to speak to a Miss Alice Crawford, the daughter of Doctor Crawford, who used to practise in Bruthen."

The woman slowly straightened and turned to see whoever was addressing her. He could see that she had been quite a beauty but was now drawn and pale. *Not long for this world*, he thought as she haltingly walked towards him.

"I am indeed Alice Crawford, daughter of Doctor Crawford. What business might you have with me?" she said.

He had been dreading this moment. How was he going to explain the strange events at his house and his notion that somehow her father was the cause of mysterious problems that any sensible person would regard as ridiculous? But after he'd introduced himself and told her he was now the tenant of her father's old surgery and house in Bruthen, she politely stopped him with a wave of her hand and said he must be tired after travelling all that way and invited him in for refreshments. She asked if he would take her arm as her balance was not what it once was. He sensed she was about to reveal information that had eluded him, and he offered her his arm, and together they walked into the house.

Seated together in the richly decorated front room, Miss Crawford arranged for her housekeeper to bring tea and cake. She sat rigidly upright in her cushioned chair, and Bill couldn't help noticing an expression of pain on her face. The housekeeper brought her some powders with a glass of water before serving tea. Much to his relief, he didn't have to explain his reason for calling. Miss Crawford said he was obviously concerned about something to do with her father, so she embarked on the family story—the doctor's story.

"My father was an exceptional medical student and established a lucrative practice in Melbourne," she said. "But the Spanish influenza outbreak in 1919 took its toll on him. He worked long hours tending to the sick and trying to find some form of treatment. It was no surprise he had a breakdown, so in the early 1920s the family moved to Bruthen— to the quiet of the country to allow him to recover. And recover he did, but all the time he worked in the laboratory he'd put together in the small room next to the surgery. But one day, he unexpectedly ordered us to pack up as soon as possible, and that's when we moved to Prahran. His nerves deteriorated once again as he locked himself away, searching for a treatment for the flu. He saw patients still, but many complained about his treatments and incessant injections. Then, one night, he summoned us to the surgery; he was agitated and raving that finally he had found a treatment. He ordered everyone to line up and injected each of us with a yellowish fluid he'd concocted, treating himself last. For some reason, he only injected a small amount into me, perhaps believing me too frail for a large dose. Soon, my mother and sister complained of pains in their joints and slumped down into chairs. I felt terrible joint pains and had difficulty breathing and squatted on the floor. I woke up in the Alfred Hospital, drifting between life and death for several days before finally regaining some measure of health. But I had been seriously weakened—mind and body—by my father's medical experiment. The hospital matron told me the awful news about my family, and that almost finished me. I was heartbroken. Father's investments provided well enough for my material needs, and I stayed in the family house under the care of an elderly aunt. Now I've a housekeeper to look after me."

The baker thought about the injections and the treatment the doctor had hoped to develop. He realised for the first time the doctor was a healer—a man of compassion trying to alleviate suffering. He had worked himself to madness and death, taking most of his family with him.

As if reading his thoughts, Miss Crawford said, "I very much loved my father: the best of men and a wonderful doctor but one whose energy and ambition brought about tragedy."

"And there was something essentially unfair in the fate that befell him," she said almost in a whisper as tears glistened in the corners of her eyes.

The baker recalled the two diamonds that had been plaguing him, and he tried to think of some way of getting Miss Crawford's assistance with the riddle. In the end, he simply came out with it and asked her if two diamonds meant anything to her. She thought for a moment and shook her head. But then she asked him to help her stand and lead her to the bookshelf in a recess in the far wall.

"Take down the three thick volumes with dark blue covers," she instructed. "They were father's notebooks. I have not studied them in any detail, but perhaps there are some annotations that might mean something to you."

The baker started to leaf through a volume and saw that the small, tightly written notes of the doctor were in chronological order, so he quickly sought out the volume that covered the time he had spent in Bruthen. He found an entry for March 1922, but it was just a jumble of symbols and abbreviations. But one word was clear: "Lamberts." The baker held the volume so Miss Crawford could see it and perhaps decipher its meaning. Her face reddened, and she appeared to bite on her bottom lip as she read the entry before raising her eyes, signifying to the baker she'd seen enough with a wave of her hand.

"The Lamberts were patients of my father," she said. "I vaguely remember them: twin brothers, eccentric hermits. Father took a special interest in them, and he often visited their house in the bush way out of Bruthen." She paused, then said, "We left Bruthen shortly after the entry in the volume."

But Miss Crawford's demeanour had changed. She was now agitated and nervous. The baker noticed a steam of tears coming from her eyes. In a soft, barely audible voice, she said, "I am feeling unwell. These giddy spells come without warning."

The baker called the housekeeper, who brought some kind of tonic and a glass of water. He felt dreadful and thought he had upset her somehow, but after a while, she regained her composure and said she needed to rest—meaning, the visit was over. The baker offered his thanks, and as the housekeeper was seeing him out, Miss Crawford called him back. She was unsteady on her feet and a little breathless.

"There were three Lambert brothers; the eccentric twins had a younger brother, a scientist who conducts research at the University of Melbourne in Carlton," she said. "I heard Father speak of him, but I don't know if he is still at the university. Perhaps if he is still there, he could give you some assistance." Then she slowly lowered herself into a chair, her eyes closed, and she fell asleep.

The tram was heading back to the city as the baker sat chatting to the same conductor he'd talked with earlier. He didn't say anything about his conversation with Miss Crawford but let the conductor know her health was delicate. But his main concern was how to get to the University of Melbourne and find the other Lambert brother.

"Listen here," said the conductor. "I know every laneway in Melbourne, so you just stay on this tram, get off at Grattan Street, and walk to the gatehouse, and the porter will help you. I'll show you the way."

A short time later, the university porter personally escorted the baker to the study of Professor Lambert in the physics building. He knocked on the door and heard a gruff "Come" shouted from inside. As he opened the door, he again thought what on earth he could say to present himself—this time to a professor—and ask some questions without making a fool of himself. So again, he just came out with it by introducing himself and saying he was trying to find out some information about a Doctor Crawford, who had practised in Bruthen some years ago, because, well, he just really needed to know something about the man whose former house he now occupied. Professor Lambert was a tall, slender man, austere in appearance, with high protruding cheekbones. His bald head was partially rimmed with the darkest of black hair, and his piercing pale blue eyes made Bill uncomfortable. He waved his visitor to a seat.

"And what might Doctor Crawford have to do with me?" he asked.

Bill explained he had visited the doctor's daughter in Prahran and had found out he'd treated his brothers.

Reflecting quietly for a short time, the stern-faced professor began a monologue, all the time looking out into a courtyard through the leadlight window.

"Yes, I recall my brothers were indeed under the care of a doctor and apparently derived considerable benefit from his treatment. They wrote to me about the doctor on the infrequent occasions they made contact." Bill listened closely as the professor told him about his brothers.

"You need to understand my brothers were reclusive men: Christian mystics who followed the ways of the ancient desert fathers by isolating themselves from society and devoutly practising their faith," the professor explained. "Often, they looked to the night sky for signs—comets and shooting stars—which they interpreted according to their own particular beliefs. But their foundation was strict religious observance and the exacting performance of rituals known best to themselves and generations long dead."

The professor mused as to why he was a professor and not a mystic. He couldn't explain why he had taken a different path from his brothers, but to be sure, they were deeply religious men who understood the universe differently from him.

The professor stood up and paced around his study, saying he had not seen or heard from his brothers for many years. It was not unusual for them to seclude themselves for a year or two, getting their meagre supplies at different places so nobody really got to know them or their movements. But several years ago, after a prolonged period without contact, he travelled to their bush hut miles out of Bruthen. The place was covered in dust and cobwebs, and animals had obviously been rummaging around inside. Their clothes and a few possessions were still there, along with a small library of tattered religious tracts, but they were nowhere to be found. He reported them as missing persons to the police at Bairnsdale, but when they made enquiries, it was soon established the brothers were strange, reclusive men and not well-known in the district. The police said they might have moved elsewhere without informing their brother so they wouldn't get involved any further in what might be a disagreement in the family.

"And that's where the matter rests," the professor concluded. He made it known to the baker that he knew no more and that he was scheduled to meet some colleagues. Bill stood to leave, but noticing a blackboard with figures chalked on it, turned to the professor and asked whether the symbol of two diamonds meant anything to him. He took up a piece of chalk and drew the diamonds on the board. The professor studied the sketch disinterestedly and said it was just two diamond shapes; it had no meaning for him.

Bill tried to focus on kneading the dough, but his mind was racing, trying to find some meaning in the information he had gained in Melbourne. He was relieved when the latch of the side gate sounded, and Joe shuffled into the bakehouse. The baker had told Joe little about his visit to Melbourne, making out he had some business with a bank, which was not altogether untrue as he was trying to establish how much he could borrow if a bakery business came on the market.

As Joe sat quietly at the table looking through a newspaper, Bill tentatively asked, "What do you know about the Lambert brothers?" He quickly qualified his question by saying he'd heard mention of them recently and was curious.

Joe looked up and thought for a while, then said, "I've a vague recollection of two brothers by that name from years ago—real loners they were." He recalled coming across them in the bush way out of Bruthen when he had gone camping for a couple days by himself as he sometimes did. "They were dressed in long coats, but mostly I remember they had large gold crosses hanging from their necks," Joe said, screwing up his face in an attempt to recall more about the encounter. "They didn't say anything much at all, so I tramped away and never saw them again. I learned their name from the general store owner up the track at Ensay. Queer as bandicoots." And with that, he let out a huge yawn and bid his brother good night.

The latch on the side gate went again soon after, and the baker expected to see Joe returning. Maybe he'd left something behind. He heaved a sigh of relief when the priest appeared, eager to know what he'd found out in Melbourne. As they sat at the table, Bill gave a detailed account of his meetings with the doctor's daughter and the professor while the priest listened intently. With his tale completed, Bill opened up, exasperated and frustrated beyond all measure.

"For all I've found out in Melbourne, I'm no closer to solving the problem," he complained. He confided in the priest that even on the train back to Bruthen, he had dozed off several times and saw the familiar two diamonds dancing around and a vision of someone who looked like his father.

The priest stopped him rambling by raising his hand and said, "Now is the time to calmly take stock of all the information we have before us." And in the priest's view, it came down to four things: the doctor, the Lamberts, the two diamonds and the baker's father.

"That's precious little to go on. There's nothing linking them," the baker protested. "And as for the two diamonds, God knows what it means."

The priest smiled and said, "Indeed, God most certainly knows, but it is up to you to discern the meaning, and how the diamonds relate to the doctor and the Lamberts and your father, and what significance all this might have."

Time was moving on, and the baker had to get back to work. But the priest, as he left, told the baker to quieten his mind as best he could and listen to his inner self, for that's where the answer would be found.

Late next morning, Bill sat at his kitchen table, tired but with an unusually calm mind. He hadn't felt this relaxed in quite a while, light-hearted and with a strong sense of inner peace as he breathed deeply. He wondered what had brought about this peaceful state but resolved to use the time wisely now that he could focus properly. He took a sheet of writing paper and a pencil and noted down all the facts he had before him: the doctor and his daughter, the noises from the doctor's rooms, Frank Davis, Mrs Erskine, the three Lambert brothers, and his father. He took a separate sheet and drew the two diamonds, then placed his work before himself and reviewed each item, alert to any movements coming from within. He recalled his daughters had been playing with a deck of cards before they'd headed off to Mansfield. He took the pack down from the shelf and slipped the cards out of their box, and the top card—as he suspected—the two of diamonds.

He maintained his contemplation for several minutes, but his mind soon wandered. He recalled an article he had read in a magazine at the Mechanics Institute about an English mathematician who had been working on a notoriously difficult problem that had stubbornly remained unsolved for centuries despite the best minds in Europe pondering it. The Englishman's years of methodical research had also yielded nothing, but he persisted. Then, one day, on a visit to London, just as he was about to cross a busy road, he suddenly had the feeling the solution would appear to him as he crossed. And that's what happened: the tumblers that had been turning fruitlessly in his head for years fell into place, and the solution became apparent. What had been there all the time as a random and meaningless equation transmuted—to the mathematician's great relief—into an elegant, recognisable pattern that was obviously the solution and would be simple to explain to those people familiar with higher-level mathematics. Bill envied the Englishman and admired his persistence. Yet his own problem, apparently sketched on the sheets of paper before him, was mute, holding tight to its secret, if indeed it had one. He became aware of his weariness and started to stand up to head off to bed for what he hoped would be a deep and restful sleep. As he stood, he glanced once again at the two diamonds, side by side, but suddenly saw them anew. No, they were not just two diamonds, but something else as well—an M sitting on top of a W—M W. And he knew immediately what it meant, and he cursed himself for being so stupid because he knew full well where he had seen M W before—the sign fixed over the entrance to his father's mine at Mount Welcome. The recognition sent a wave of relief through him, body and mind. Whatever the cause of the strange events in his life, somehow, the Mount Welcome mine held the key, and that's where something unknown had been directing him all along.

———————————

The baker knocked up Hodges and asked to borrow his horse and trap and said to just trust him; he had some urgent business.

"Frankly, Bill, your strange behaviour is beginning to get on my goat," Hodges said. But such was the respect he had for his friend and employee that he had no hesitation in helping him hitch up the horse. Bill had brought along a hurricane lantern and some tools that he put in the large box used to carry bread for delivery. Hodges watched, puzzled, as his friend, atop the trap, headed up the Bruthen hill for God knows where.

Moving along at a good clip, Bill headed past the cemetery, looking for the turnoff to Deptford and Mount Welcome. Dark clouds were building in the eastern sky, and the wind was strengthening—sure signs of heavy weather. He turned off the main road onto the Engineers Track and hoped it was passable. He hadn't been out this way for years, at least not as far as Mount Welcome. The gum trees were thrashing about in a macabre dance in the stiffening breeze; dead twigs fell onto his path, and the sound of cracking timber came from the bush. The afternoon light was becoming leaden, and shadows made seeing the track difficult. Just as he was about to pass the last of the houses along the track, he saw a dark figure looming, standing motionless some forty yards before him. He reined in the horse and narrowed his eyes, trying to make out who it might be. As he came to a stop, the priest walked alongside the trap, looking up expectantly at the baker.

"Good day to you. I've been offering pastoral care to one of the locals," the priest said, but the baker quickly cut him off.

"Listen, Father. I've finally tumbled the meaning of the two diamonds. It's an M on top of a W—my father's old mine at Mount Welcome," said the baker triumphantly. "And that's where I'm headed."

The priest gave a smile of satisfaction. "Shove over. I'm coming along too," he said.

The baker warned him it would probably be a rough trip, what with the weather and rutted road, but the priest had already taken his seat, eager to get going. Bill soon had the trap up to speed and pushed along the rough track as black wallabies darted across their path and the foul weather closed in.

Over an hour later, they neared Mount Welcome, and Bill slowed the horse, looking for signs of the narrow path leading to the mine. Lightning flashes illuminated the dense bush on all sides as the priest watched Bill jump down from the trap and walk along the track, peering into the bush.

"I've found the way in. Bring the trap closer," the baker yelled.

When the priest arrived, he saw an overgrown, rough-stepped path heading up the mountainside.

The rain held off as the two men gathered up the lantern and tools and made their way carefully up the steep, slippery path. They reached level ground, and Bill assisted the priest for the last few steps by taking his hand. It felt like a lump of ice, and Bill almost broke his grip before managing to pull the priest up the last step. "Stick your hands in your pockets, Father, and warm them up," he advised. But the priest ignored him, eager to press on.

Before them stood the boarded-up entrance to a mine, over which hung a small sign—Mt Welcome—with the M capitalised large over the equally large W. Bill quietly chided himself for not understanding the meaning of the two diamonds sooner, but the priest smiled knowingly at him, telling him to be easy on himself. Bill's dreadful boyhood memories of the place flooded back; his father's filthy curses at finding no gold and screaming abuse at Joe, who'd been made to work carrying rock out of the mine. It was a horrible place. No wonder he'd stayed away from it for so long.

The priest was all for getting into the mine immediately, but the baker stood still, looking at the timbers across the entrance. "Someone has been in the mine since my father closed it," he said. "Someone unaccustomed to using tools."

"How could you know such a thing?" the priest asked.

"The nails holding some of the timber planks are bent over," Bill explained. My father never bent a nail; he hammered them home straight. Only someone inexperienced would do that. You'd get a clip around the ear if you bent a nail around my father. I reckon someone has removed the timbers and tried to put them back as if nothing had happened."

Bill set to work with a small crowbar and levered off a couple of the planks—enough for them to get in. He lit the lantern, and it cast its faint light down the mine shaft, hewn through solid rock. Streaks of white quartz appeared in the rock after they had walked hunched over for a few yards. *The promise of gold*, thought Bill. But it was a false promise for this mine.

The main shaft went in quite a way, and Bill noticed the timbers were still in good condition, admitting to himself that his father really did know how to build a safe mine. But when they reached the end—a solid wall of rock—they found nothing out of the ordinary. The baker cast the light from the lantern into every corner and crack in the shaft but saw nothing unexpected. He looked despairingly at the priest, who just shook his head, unsure of how to help. Then, the baker took stock of the situation. If someone unaccustomed to manual work had entered the mine, where would they most likely go? Bill and the priest backtracked towards the opening, and it was there they spotted a small shaft leading off the main one at about knee height, just big enough for a man to ease himself through. It was an exploratory shaft, probably dug to follow a seam of quartz. Bill crawled in on his hands and knees, placing the lantern before him. The small shaft led into a larger chamber, only shoulder height but with enough room to stand bent over. He cast the light around, but nothing much appeared except in one corner, where he saw what looked like a pile of old rope and rags that must have been left behind. He edged his way closer to inspect it, and in the dusty rags, he made out two human skulls staring back at him with terrible, toothy smiles, their eye sockets seeming to focus on his every movement. He reeled backwards in fright, falling over and trying to get his breath.

"For God's sake, come in, quickly," he called to the priest and held the lantern with a trembling hand to light his way.

The priest scurried into the chamber and saw the baker, white-faced, slumped on the ground. Bill stood up and held the lantern so as to direct its light towards the pile of rags. The priest straightaway saw the skulls and immediately crossed himself and mumbled a prayer. The two men, hunched over, walked closer to examine the remains. The pile of rags was, in fact, two suits of clothes, and the skulls were part of two intact human skeletons. But the skulls were covered with a parchment-like translucent skin, as were the hand bones extending from the sleeves of their ragged jackets covering the rib cages. Stretched out before them, the two skeletons seemed to be holding each other's hands.

Bill was shocked at the parchment-like skin that covered the skulls. It seemed unnatural and made them look as if they were still alive in some macabre way. But the priest reassured him. "I've seen remains like these before in Dublin in the crypt of St Michan's Church—a crusader's remains, no less," he said. "The dry air preserved the skin and bones for hundreds of years. This mine must have the same conditions."

Bill steadied himself and knelt near the skeletons, holding the lantern close to the skulls. A glint of reflected light caught his eye, coming from just under the jawbone of the skeleton nearest him. Carefully reaching into the rags, he turned up a gold cross, still attached to the neckbones with a solid chain. The priest crossed himself, and the baker let go of the cross and said, "The truth is revealed: these are the remains of the Lambert brothers. My brother Joe told me about their crosses."

The priest took up a position on the other side of one of the skeletons and placed his hand in the upper pocket of its ragged coat. He pulled out a small Bible and, opening the cover, saw a name neatly written on the end cover: Francis Lambert. He showed Bill then returned the Bible to where he'd found it.

Bill again became overwhelmed by their discovery and sat back on the ground, surveying the remains in silence, as did the priest. Then, something on the rock wall near the outstretched arm of one of the skeletons caught his attention. He quickly moved the lantern closer and saw scrawled writing on the rock, obviously made with a sharp piece of stone that lay near the hand.

"Consecrated ground. God forgive doctor," Bill read aloud.

He looked at the priest, imploring him to explain what it all meant. The priest settled back and sat on the ground, nodding his head slowly, figuring things out.

"Here's what I think happened," said the priest. "It was Doctor Crawford himself who brought the Lamberts here because he did something he thought had killed them and wanted to cover his tracks. That inexperienced person who'd opened and closed the mine, that was the doctor—medically clever with his hands, but no carpenter, just as you said. He laid the brothers together, perhaps tending to them as they died from God knows what. But obviously, he left before one of the brothers had passed, and it was he who managed somehow to scrawl that note."

"We'd better head back to town to get the police," Bill said.

But the priest was quick to his feet and stood at the exit blocking the way out. He demanded Bill's attention and asked to be heard out. "The police or any officials, for that matter, have no business here," he said. "The Lamberts and the doctor are dead, and no good will come from bumbling legal men trying to piece together events of years ago: events they could never truly understand. There is far more at stake here than conducting some half-baked inquest and completing the proper paperwork. The Lamberts and the doctor must find peace and have a blockage removed to enable them to move on. That's what's been behind the strange occurrences in your house—the dreams and the two diamonds. It would be a travesty of universal justice to prolong their suffering by having the Lamberts' remains moved to some pathologist's laboratory where they'll be abused and forgotten. They were devout men, and their deepest wish was clear: burial in consecrated ground. That's where the doctor made a great mistake—a mistake he has been trying to correct for many years."

Bill was hesitant, and even though he understood everything the priest said was right, it felt wrong taking the law into their own hands. But the priest was adamant and as he thought about it, Bill was swayed to his view. He knew the Lamberts had to be removed from this dreadful mine—a God-forsaken place permeated by his father's filthy language and oaths and his greed for gold.

"Alright," Bill conceded. "What should we do?"

The wind howled outside the mine, but the rain held off as Bill and the priest carried the remains of the Lamberts in a tarpaulin to the storage tray on the trap. Bill resealed the mine entrance, taking care to straighten all the bent nails before hammering them home correctly. Then he turned the trap around and headed back to Bruthen, wondering what the priest had in mind. The priest sat quietly for a time before he turned to Bill to describe how they should proceed.

"We'll head to the consecrated ground at the Bruthen cemetery," the priest said slowly. "I know for sure that the burial of a deceased Catholic gentleman is to take place there tomorrow: the grave has already been dug. So, we'll bury the Lamberts at the bottom of that grave, thereby fulfilling their wish. Then the other burial will take place, the grave sealed, and one problem in the universe will be finally laid to rest."

Bill didn't have to think about it. He knew the priest was right, so he clipped the horse to a fair trot and hoped there would be no one at the cemetery in the early evening.

The cemetery would certainly be deserted because, just before the baker and priest arrived, torrents of rain poured down from the dark clouds that were crowding in from the east. As they drove in, the priest pointed to a plot in the Catholic section where a tarpaulin covered a low frame with a mound of dirt to one side. Bill eased the trap to a stop, checking that nobody was about and taking up a shovel from a canvas bag near a mound of dirt, lifted a flap on the tarpaulin, and slid down into the grave. The earth was loose and easily worked, so Bill, labouring under cover, shovelled out a good eighteen inches of dirt from the grave—enough to conceal the two skeletons. Then, working in driving rain, they carefully removed the remains of the Lamberts from the trap and arranged them side by side in the grave. Bill completed the task by covering them with dirt and restored the area to pretty much as they had found it. The base of the grave looked as it did when they arrived. Nobody would see any evidence of its new tenants, and there was plenty of room for the coffin of the Catholic gentleman that would lie above the Lamberts.

"It's time to go. Our work is done," said Bill.

But the priest said they were not quite finished. The priest and the baker, standing side by side, paid their final respects. "God's work and that of His servants is finally done to bring peace to troubled souls," said the priest as he gave his blessing.

They headed down the Bruthen hill and turned into town, where the priest alighted. Looking at Bill, wide-eyed and with a soft smile traced on his lips, he blessed him and his family, then bid him goodnight. Bill watched as the priest walked towards his lodgings, the heavy rain beginning to abate.

He returned the horse and trap to Hodges, who, seeing his friend's state, told him to go home and get out of his wet things before he caught pneumonia, saying he would take care of the stabling. "God knows what you've been up to," Hodges growled.

Bill smiled and thought if only Hodges knew how close to the mark his words were.

Rugged up in his dressing gown and with a pot of hot tea and bread and jam before him, Bill sat at the kitchen table listening to the last of the rain pass. He could sense the house was now silent and perhaps had a feeling of warmth and peace about it. But this house would never welcome his family again as its tenants—that much he knew. He headed off to bed, deeply content with his day's work, knowing that the problem that had beset his family had finally been laid to rest.

The train pulled into the station, and Bill's daughters waved frantically from their carriage and soon ran down the platform to hug their father. He picked them up and went to help Sarah unload the bags and cases and enjoy her cuddles. Joe had brought along a large car to get them all home, and it was a chaotic and happy scene as they sped along, all trying to talk at the same time, with Joe tooting the horn freely at anyone they came across.

Before they reached the turnoff to the doctor's house, Joe slowed the car and headed down a side street just past the church. They pulled up at a small grey weatherboard cottage with iron lacework around the veranda—Mrs Reilly's house. Sarah looked quizzically at Bill.

"It's all Mrs Erskine's work," he said. "You know Mrs Reilly has been widowed for years and is having trouble coping with the housework and cooking, even for herself. Well, Mrs Erskine had a word with her and suggested she spend some time with her daughter in Sale. She agreed, but more importantly, let the house to us, and at a very good rent, I might add."

Sarah and girls looked around the neat and spotlessly clean house. Mrs Erskine and Edgar had been in several days before and scoured it spotlessly clean. Bill and Joe had moved everything out of the doctor's place and set it up perfectly in the new house. The relief on the faces of Sarah and the girls was palpable; no more doctor's house and now a cosy cottage in the town proper, well away from the place they despised and feared.

"And the doctor's house?" Sarah whispered to Bill.

"It's been boarded up, and the agent says there's talk of demolishing it. I don't know the full story, but good riddance," he replied.

The fortunes of Bill and his family were again looking up. A bakehouse with a house attached was for sale in Buchan—a good business at a reasonable price. Bill made some enquires with his bank in Bairnsdale, and eventually, a loan was approved. Sarah was not entirely convinced it was a good move; she didn't want to raise her daughters in a remote place like Buchan. But Bill told her the scenic caves and camping reserve were attracting a lot of tourists, so they would enjoy good business as well as interesting visitors.

Sarah thought about it long and hard and finally gave her husband an ultimatum. "Five years and not a single day more, and then we move to Melbourne," she demanded.

Bill accepted her terms but quietly hoped that Gippsland would always be their home.

Some weeks later, a letter arrived for him with a solicitor's business name printed on the envelope. When he opened it, he found a short typewritten note attached to an envelope. It was from a lawyer acting for Miss Alice Crawford of Ivy Street, Prahran, and said that Miss Crawford had recently died, but before her demise, she had instructed that the attached letter should be forwarded to the addressee as soon as possible after her death. He quickly opened the second envelope, which contained an elegant handwritten letter addressed to him.

Dear Mr. William O'Connell,

This message will find you after blessed death has claimed me. Yet, as I approach the end, I have but one regret: that I was not entirely honest with you when we met and discussed my father. Please accept my sincerest apologies and know that I was trying to respect the memory of my dear father.

He was a complex man and possessed great kindness. I can now tell you that he kept a special diary of his time at Bruthen, and it contains many entries about the Lambert brothers—far more than the scrap of detail in the journal you saw during your visit. It seems Father was intrigued by their religious practices and mystical views. After we moved to Melbourne, I can remember him saying that the churchmen know nothing of God's creation - only the truly devout, like the Lamberts, have such knowledge. He recorded that he often spent time at the Lamberts' bush home discussing such matters. But there is something rather terrible recorded in his notes as well. The Lamberts, out of compassion for others, agreed to submit themselves to father's medical experiments to find a treatment for influenza. You will, of course, remember me telling you Father was obsessed with finding a treatment after his experiences during the influenza outbreak in 1919.

I am leading up to one entry in particular where he wrote "… the dosage must have been too strong. They were immediately rendered unconscious, and after a short time, I could detect no vital signs, so I laid their remains in a place where, hopefully, many years will pass before they are discovered, or perhaps they will decay away entirely. God forgive me."

Mr. O'Connell, I know no more than that, but perhaps it has fallen to you to find the place where the Lamberts were taken and see that a proper burial takes place. Yes, perhaps that's God's will.

In closing, I can only say that my father was a good man trying his best to relieve suffering.

I trust this letter to your discretion.

Yours faithfully,

Miss Alice Crawford.

Bill read the note a second time, then threw it into the fire of the kitchen stove. His business with the doctor was done.

Joe had driven his brother into Bairnsdale in his new car to finalise the paperwork for the business at Buchan. After his appointment at the bank, Bill had some time to spare while Joe attended to business of his own, so he wandered down Main Street to St Mary's Catholic Church. He admired its commanding presence and wondered whether its red bricks had been made by his uncle, who'd been a local manufacturer. On the spur of the moment, he thought he might pay his respects to Father Doolan. There was nobody inside the church when he entered, and he stared at the colourful murals of biblical scenes but grimaced when he saw the depictions of souls abandoned in hell. Presently, an overweight priest appeared, and Bill asked after Father Doolan. The priest went out, and soon, a tall, young man of thickset appearance came in.

"Hello, I am Father Doolan. How can I be of assistance?" he said in a broad Australian accent.

"I'm sorry. I'm looking for another priest by the name of Father Doolan," Bill stammered and instantly realised how foolish he sounded.

The young priest assured him that he was the only Father Doolan in these parts and, indeed, the whole of the diocese. Bill was dumbfounded and couldn't find words to express himself but seeing that the priest was becoming impatient and annoyed, he mumbled his apologies and left.

Joe swung the car around in the street and, catching sight of his brother walking out of St Mary's, tooted the horn and pulled up.

"What the hell are you doing in the church of those bloody Romans?" Joe caustically asked as his brother climbed into the car.

Bill didn't answer, and Joe, in a huff, crunched the car into gear and dropped the clutch so it took off with a jolt. Bill turned his head for another look at the church, and there, standing near the main entrance, waving his hand and smiling, was the little Irish priest who had shared his adventures and been his adviser. The baker looked closer, and the figure slowly vanished through the solid wooden door—a door that was shut. His face betrayed his utter incomprehension, and with his mouth hanging open, he turned to Joe, hoping he had seen the priest too.

"What the hell is wrong with you?" Joe asked gruffly. "You look like you've just seen a ghost."

The baker distractedly asked Joe what he'd said and then smiled hugely before breaking into laughter.

"High time we got ourselves home," Bill declared to his puzzled brother.

The Baker of Gippsland

Buchan

February 1942

Even as war engulfs the world, an unresolved tragedy close to home requires an unsuspecting country baker, guided by mysterious signs, to settle past wrongs.

———————————————

The baker sat at the kitchen table listening to the midday news on the radio while Sarah ladled freshly made green tomato pickles into jars. The announcer's voice was sombre: "Darwin has been bombed by Japanese aircraft. An unknown number of civilians and sailors on ships in the harbour have been killed. More attacks are expected."

The news was getting worse as each day passed.

Bill solemnly said to his wife, almost in a whisper—"A week ago, Singapore fell. Last December, the American fleet was bombed to hell at Pearl Harbour. I hate to say it, but everything is pointing to a Japanese invasion of Australia."

Sarah was subdued and brooding but finished the pickles and made a pot of tea. They sat quietly, thinking what might become of their family and their country. Looming large in Sarah's mind was the newspaper articles she'd read years ago about the atrocities the Japanese army committed in China. Women and girls raped—mutilated with bayonets—the butchered bodies piled into grotesque heaps before being doused with petrol and set alight.

Bill had been confident the British would come to Australia's aid, but that was now unlikely as they were under siege from German bombing. And they were facing an invasion of their own after the fall of France. America was Australia's only hope—Prime Minister Curtin made that clear in *The Herald* newspaper just after Christmas. And Bill had another concern close to his heart: his younger brother, Cyril, had been captured when the Germans invaded Greece and was now a prisoner of war.

Sarah broke the silence. "If the Japs get anywhere near Buchan, I'll drown the girls and myself in the swimming pool up near the caves—I won't have them going through rape and torture."

"Stop talking rot—the girls might hear; they're playing just outside," Bill chided. "Besides, the Japanese are a long way from Buchan."

Sarah quickly rebutted him. "You mark my words. If the Japs get anywhere near here, I'll take matters into my own hands."

They both stared into their teacups. Bill tried to ease the tension. "Look, it's unlikely Emperor Hirohito has told his troops 'Whatever you do, take Buchan.' None of them has even heard of the place. Christ, most Australians don't know it exists, or they didn't until the caves opened for tourists."

"Stop making a joke of it all," Sarah snapped, and Bill relented as he again realised the precarious situation they now faced.

―――――――

The family's move to Buchan six years ago had been a rewarding new start. Finally, a business of their own, and it had exceeded all expectations. Their new house with an attached bakehouse and shop meant Bill was working close to home, and Sarah could take care of the shop. The bakery itself was well-equipped, and its wood-fired oven produced golden-crusted bread with a distinctive, soft, fluffy crumb. The real secret, though, was that Bill was making his own yeast—forced on him at first by wartime rationing, but now a skill he had crafted into an art form.

Tourists thronged in from Melbourne to see the limestone caves and enjoy the novelty of camping in tents. Locals and tourists alike praised Bill's bread and buns, and his idea of home delivery by horse and cart had bolstered sales. Another daughter had arrived—Beatrice— making three. The family had been well and truly accepted as locals, and there was no shortage of social activities—card nights, and tennis on the weekends. Helen and Ruthie, the two oldest children, had settled in at the local school, and Sarah enjoyed the regular meetings of the Country Women's Association. She was even regarded as an expert cook because she could whip up a batch of scrumptious scones and jam with whipped cream in a few minutes.

Bill had proved he could run a successful business—to himself and his wife, and even to his haughty father, who was now whiling away his old age down near Koo Wee Rup. Success was a good feeling—being respected around town and having money in the bank—but now, it was in jeopardy as war intensified in Europe and the Japanese took control of the Pacific.

Most of the young men of Buchan had enlisted in the army; even the caves were closing to tourists because all the guides had signed up. In any case, tourists were no longer visiting in anywhere near the numbers they once did, so demand for bread and baked goods was well down. Still, people had to eat, so he enjoyed a good trade among the locals.

Bill's thoughts often went back to the frightening experiences he and his family had endured at Bruthen years earlier when some unseen presence in their house had made life miserable. It was finally put to rest when he found the cause of the problem with the assistance of a mysterious Irish priest. But lately, the Bruthen experience came more to mind as vague and persistent dreams once again disturbed his sleep.

Now he regularly dreamt about falling—falling off a cliff, even falling off the cart he used to deliver bread. He knew the dreams had some underlying message—this much he had learnt from the priest years ago. So, he avoided high places and took care when mounting his cart for bread deliveries—that was about all he could think of. But in his heart, he knew the dreams carried some subtler, deeper message.

He sensed, and in some ways, hoped, the mysterious Irish priest might return and help him to interpret his dreams. But the priest had not appeared, and Bill bumbled about, trying to figure out the meaning of his dreams by himself.

Again, he felt lost and anxious, fearing the events of Bruthen might be about to repeat themselves and that he might again be separated from his family. But thankfully, it seemed that he was the only one having these dreams, unlike Bruthen when everyone was plagued with nightmares.

The war spurred the people of Buchan into defensive action, and they'd formed a local volunteer militia. Most of the men in town and on surrounding farms not eligible for military service had joined, and an ex-Great War sergeant, Jack Jones, became the officer-in-charge. Training exercises took place a couple of evenings each week and some weekends. The volunteers had to supply their own guns, which was no problem as most of the locals were keen rabbit shooters—something of a necessity in these days of food rationing. But there was little actual shooting at the exercises because of the cost of ammunition, and it was in short supply. So, they mostly focussed on taking up defensive positions near roads and finding places that could be used as vantage points.

Bill felt a little guilty because he enjoyed the training exercises immensely. They got him away from the bakery, and there was plenty of good humour to be had among his fellow volunteers. He had been assigned to marking up military reconnaissance maps with points of interest: defensive positions, lookouts, and water sources. He did it by himself and enjoyed trekking around the bush, breathing in the cleansing fragrance of the gum trees. It immediately took him back to the happy times of his childhood in Deptford when he went exploring in the bush with his brother Joe.

At one of the training sessions, he had been released from muster to check a remote area about a mile or so from base camp. Sergeant Jones and the rest of the men were practising their shooting, but due to the shortage of ammunition, they'd been told to yell "Bang" when they fired a shot from their empty guns. Bill couldn't see the point and would have fallen about laughing in any case, so he was glad of another assignment.

He slowly headed down an overgrown track—really, a path he'd picked out between the bushes. It was north of the caves reserve, and as he surveyed the immensity of the surrounding dense bushland, he realised it could easily shelter an entire army—the whole Japanese army.

So much for defending Buchan, he thought.

Suddenly, a feeling came over him: a feeling that he was not alone. Perhaps it was one of his mates playing a joke. He swivelled around but saw nothing, yet the feeling persisted. The sun had almost dropped below the horizon, its last rays illuminating a clearing not far from the baker. He turned to face it, and immediately his body stiffened, and he was breathless. Squinting his eyes, he barely made out a form that looked like a man—an aboriginal man with streaks of white paint across his chest and arms. He carried a long wooden spear and raised it as if pointing to something. Then, in a final glimmer of sunlight, the figure disappeared, and the baker could find no evidence of it even though he searched the clearing. The light was fading quickly, and he edged his way cautiously back to the main track, wondering all the time what the hell he had just seen.

The volunteers were starting to head home by the time he made it back to the pavilion, where they assembled before training sessions. He handed his reconnaissance map to Sergeant Jones, saying he had marked some good water sources and places of concealment for ten or more men. Then he noticed one of the volunteers, a local farmer he hardly knew, George Davies, seated on a wooden bench, smoking a cigarette, and in no hurry to go anywhere. Davies had fixed the baker firmly in his gaze, and it seemed as if he wanted to say something. But then he rose slowly and, with a backwards glance at the baker, headed towards the car park.

As he walked home, the baker turned over in his mind the meaning of the sudden appearance of the Aboriginal and getting the "eye" from George Davies. And his mind drifted back to the little Irish priest who had helped him solve the mysterious haunting of his house at Bruthen— the priest had advised him to look into his heart and mind for the meaning of seemingly incomprehensible messages. And these messages, if that's what they were, were certainly incomprehensible.

The Japanese had taken Burma, and the British forces were retreating to India. The radio brought only bad news these days. Bill began to more seriously consider what he would do if the Japanese arrived in Buchan. Defend the town with a shotgun? Hardly. Australia would have surrendered by then, and surrender would only bring suffering to his family—Sarah was right about that. His mind was teeming with disturbed thoughts as he slid between the sheets for his afternoon nap before baking through the night. He wondered how his brother Cyril was faring as a prisoner of war but recalled his stoical nature; he knew how to survive in tough conditions. He had, after all, survived his father's tyranny. The baker tried to relax his tall frame and settle his mind; he really needed some deep sleep to get through the night's baking. Then, there he was, walking through the dark and silent bush, a half-moon lighting his way. Underfoot was solid ground, and his boot clapped against the hard yellow clay. Then he broke into a run, and suddenly he was falling and trying with all his might to grab onto something to break his fall, but there was nothing to grasp—and, with a start, he woke up. The baker looked at his alarm clock through half-closed, tired eyes and realised he'd slept for four hours. Another falling dream had shaken him awake, just as it had several times in recent weeks. He was always falling. That was the message he had to decipher.

On his delivery rounds the next day, he dropped off two high tin loaves at Frank Morgan's house. Morgan was one of the first Europeans to thoroughly explore the caves at Buchan and had been head caretaker of the reserve when it was opened to the public for tours and camping. Although he'd retired a couple of years ago, he still spent much of his time at the caves, talking to staff and tourists. No one knew the caves like Morgan. He was sitting on his veranda when the baker arrived, who suddenly had the thought Morgan might be able to help him with his dream if he could approach it in a roundabout way.

"Good morning, Frank," the baker said as he sauntered up the steps to the veranda. "A couple of high tins for you—dark on top, just the way you like."

"G'day, Bill. I haven't long finished breakfast, but I reckon I could knock off one of those loaves right here and now," Morgan chortled. "I'd like to know your secret formula."

"Trade secret, sorry—but don't worry—I'll be baking for you for a while yet."

Frank had a reassuring smile as Bill broached the subject of the caves reserve.

"Frank, you know I'm in the militia marking out military maps with water sources and defensive positions—in the event of a Japanese invasion," the baker said. "What can you tell me about the place so I know what to look for?"

Frank shuffled in his chair and thought for a moment before replying.

"Well, the reserve is rough country all right, full of all manner of caves and holes. You'll have no problem finding plenty of hiding spots and advantageous high positions. But never forget it's dangerous country too. Crickey, when I first started exploring there, I nearly ended up falling to the bottom of a few deep caves—holes covered over with grass and bushes—holes that seemed bottomless. You'd never get out by yourself. So have a stout long staff with you wherever you go off the beaten track and poke around on the path you're taking to make sure you aren't stepping into a hole."

The baker listened closely, and he thought that maybe his dreams were telling him to beware of falling into holes and caves in the reserve. Good practical advice, but he remembered his dreams in Bruthen conveyed a cryptic message. Maybe his dreams were trying to tell him something else, something far more important.

"Did you ever see Aboriginals around the caves?" the baker asked, indirectly fishing for any information about the vision he'd experienced a couple of days earlier.

"Sure, the blackfellows know far more than anyone credits but keep it to themselves. They regard the place as sacred and spiritually powerful. They took care where they went, particularly around nightfall."

Then Morgan went quiet for a moment and looked around to see if anyone other than the baker was listening.

"It's not only the hidden holes and crevices that present a danger," he confided. "There is something eerie, fearful about the caves, as if they are inhabited by beings … from another world. I've never told anyone this, but I always made sure I was out of the reserve by nightfall. Early in my exploring days, I worked by lantern light at night, but soon stopped when I sensed the presence of something threatening—yes, not of this world. I'd see shadows darting along the cave walls, but when I tried to get a good look at them, they were gone. I wondered if I was just imagining things. Anyway, it happened too often, so I soon learnt that before the sun went down, it was time to stop exploring and head for home. The campground is fine, but not the caves. You keep this to yourself, Bill, but take care you heed my advice."

The baker agreed to keep quiet about the conversation, then continued with his deliveries, thinking about the feeling he had the other night of some unseen presence when he was in the reserve alone at nightfall. Maybe Morgan's talk about falling into holes and crevices tallied with his dreams of falling, but he doubted it. There was some deeper meaning. In any case, Morgan was right; the caves were no place to be near dusk or at night. Perhaps some presence was trying to prevent unwelcome visitors. And after his experiences in Bruthen with Doctor Crawford and the Lambert brothers, he didn't need any more excursions into the supernatural.

Bill lounged in a large armchair, yawning and replete, one Sunday afternoon after a splendid lunch of roast lamb and all the trimmings. Sarah and the kids were busy at the sewing machine with pieces of cloth and white thread all over the floor, but rather than doze off, he went out for a walk to get some air. But this was no aimless stroll... he soon set off for the place where he'd seen the painted Aboriginal a few nights ago. Retracing his steps, he came to what he thought was the path he'd taken, but it was so overgrown that he was uncertain it was leading him to the right place. There was a small rise nearby with a tree on top, so he headed there to get his bearings. It provided a good view of the surrounds, and he was able to make out the rough path he'd taken previously. Then looking down, he saw something odd—a cigarette butt that had been squashed underfoot. Picking it up, he noticed it was fresh with no signs of dampness or discolouration; it had certainly been dropped recently. It smelt of strong tobacco; it had the Capstan brand printed on it. There was a black, shrivelled up match nearby, too. The baker wondered whose it might have been, but his thoughts quickly returned to the track, and discarding the butt, he set off down the hill to a spot he had sighted.

He slackened his pace and carefully watched where he stepped as he edged his way through prickly shrubs. Craning his neck, he saw the clearing ahead. It was a small open area surrounded by trees, and a stone outcrop, rising into a cliff face, pockmarked with holes, ran along one side. The baker scrambled over it, trying to investigate some of the holes and cracks, then saw it was becoming too steep, so he retraced his steps back to safe ground. He stood looking at the cliff face and thought he could make out a path that led along the rock face into dense bush. He sat back on the trunk of a fallen tree and surveyed the scene, aware that the sun was getting lower, but there was still a good couple of hours of light remaining. There was something about this place that drew him. He felt it was holding on to a secret of some type, and he was intent on discovering its meaning. But this country was rough and dangerous; it would need more than one man to explore it, and particularly so if he decided to enter some of the holes and crevices. He remembered his brother Joe was visiting next week to check some timber he was buying for his axe-handle factory. Yes, Joe would give him a hand looking over this place; he always loved poking around in the bush and long walks.

The baker headed home while the light held. He gingerly made his way through the thick shrubs, noting landmarks and features for when he brought Joe here. Once he gained the main track, he walked quickly towards the main road and, breaking into a run, strode up a small rise that overlooked the caves reserve back toward its entrance. Motionless, he watched as a black automobile, a Ford, sped along the road and turned out of the reserve onto the main road. He thought it unusual for someone to be leaving in such a hurry as most tourists, if indeed it was a tourist, travelled slowly on the road taking in the scenic bushland beauty. For some reason, he looked down at his feet and noticed a cigarette butt ground into the dirt. Picking it up, he saw it was fresh, despite the inground dust, and still warm. It was the Capstan brand again, and the baker wondered who this smoker was, why he seemed to be following him, and did this have anything to do with the car he had seen leaving the reserve. All good questions, but he had no answers, so headed home to Sarah and the kids.

Joe arrived the next Saturday and conducted his timber buying with Fred Bell, the mill owner. As usual the negotiations always involved a blazing argument, with Joe accusing Fred of robbing him blind, and Fred countering by saying he was virtually giving his timber away at cost. Anyway, they reached a grudging truce, and a price was decided on. Joe came back to the bakery with a sly smile on his face, and the baker knew he'd got the deal he wanted.

After lunch, the baker took Joe aside. "Let's do some exploring at a place I've just discovered," he said. "Sarah and the kids are going to look at the ponies at the park down the road."

"Righto. A good walk in the bush will clear my head from all the rubbish Fred was spouting," Joe replied. "I've got some boots in the car I use when I go out shooting."

Joe was surprised when his brother appeared with a coil of rope, which he placed in a backpack along with a torch.

"Holy mackerel. Have you found another limestone cave or something?" Joe exclaimed.

"No, no. Nothing like that. I just want to look at some crevices I've seen in a cliff face in the reserve."

They set out and were soon traipsing through the thick bushland shrubs, heading towards the cliff face. Joe complained about the uneven, slippery ground when they started moving along the base of cliff face. "This is a good place to break your arm or leg. Watch your step," he advised.

The baker, ever alert, kept his eyes fixed on finding a track but paused at one spot because he found a torn piece of cloth among the stones: it looked like it was from a red checked flannel shirt. He put it in his pocket and started moving forward again.

Joe yelled he needed a break and was going to sit down for a spell. The baker pushed on, edging around a large fallen rock, losing sight of Joe. A strange feeling overcame him—a sense that something was about to happen, and he became a little unnerved. He heard a muffled sound and cocked his ear to make out its origin. It was the sound of falling water. He'd heard tell about a waterfall around here. And suddenly, it struck him—his dreams had been about the falls, not falling down a hole. Focussing on the path ahead, the baker was suddenly transfixed by the gradual appearance of a form—a human form—the Aboriginal with the streaks of paint again stood before him, his face stern and eyes looking fiercely at the baker. And again, the Aboriginal's arm pointed at some place that the baker could not quite yet see.

Looking behind him, the baker yelled to Joe to come up quickly, but when he turned to face the Aboriginal, he was gone.

Joe arrived, blustering. "What's all the fuss about?"

The baker stood dumfounded and silent. "I thought I saw something—an Aboriginal—but he's gone."

"That's for certain," Joe said, looking at his brother as if he'd gone strange.

The baker recovered himself. "Let's move up along the cliff face and see what we can find," he muttered.

They scrambled around more large rocks, then came to a place where there was a large gash in the rock face. It appeared to be the entrance to a cave. The baker was first to reach the opening, and shining his torch down into the darkness, he saw an oval-shaped tunnel descending at an angle.

Joe arrived and tentatively looked into the dark shaft, screwing up his face. "It's a bloody dark and fearful place if you ask me," he croaked, a little out of breath. "God knows what might be in there."

The baker shone the torch around all corners, but they only saw a rock wall descending gradually into darkness. "Let's tie the rope around the base of that sapling and use it to lower ourselves into the cave. And we can use it to pull ourselves out," he said, looking at Joe.

Joe was not so sure. "Just wait up a minute," he quickly instructed. "Maybe that shaft drops away vertically further down. Have you considered that? The rope wouldn't be long enough, and anyway, using a rope without proper climbing gear is beyond our capabilities."

But the baker persisted and said he would use the rope to edge his way in gradually, being alert to sudden drops. Joe grudgingly agreed and tied off one end of rope to the sapling. The baker, holding tight to the rope with the torch slung around his neck, slowly descended the incline into the cave, making sure there was solid rock underfoot before taking another step. Soon, he reached the end of the rope, but the shaft continued downward, and shining the torch around, he saw it was becoming even steeper.

The baker shouted to Joe he was coming up, and as he turned around, he saw a cigarette butt on a small ledge. He picked it up and put it in his pocket. Pulling hard on the rope, he slowly clambered back to the light and soon saw Joe peering curiously into the shaft, relieved to see his brother returning.

The baker had nothing much to report. The cave was much the same further down as it was near the entrance, maybe getting steeper. They would need a longer rope and some gloves to get a better grip on the rope, as well as a better torch.

But Joe had had enough of his brother's adventures.

"What the hell are you trying to achieve, climbing down some god-forsaken hole in the ground that might go down forever?" he yelled. "It's dangerous, and you don't have the skills or the equipment for the job."

The baker was at a loss to explain himself to Joe, but he didn't have to because Joe now gave full vent to his rage.

"You bring me out here on the pretext of having a walk in the bush, but you're not being honest with me—you are looking for something you're not telling me about," he snarled. "You're acting like you did in Bruthen years ago when you thought your house was haunted. Is that it? Are you seeing ghosts again or something?"

"Alright, if you have to know, it's just that dreams and strange feelings—and yes, visions—are telling me that something is not right … something has happened that … needs to be put right," Bill tersely replied. "I don't expect you to understand—you're a practical man— but try to see it from my point of view, for once in your life."

"Be buggered," Joe snorted angrily as he wound up the rope, meaning the expedition was over. "I'll tell you something, Bill. Do you want Sarah and the kids leaving you again like in Bruthen because that's what is going to happen if you keep up this bloody ghosts and visions nonsense."

Joe's words jolted the baker into silence, and the memory of the loneliness and fear he felt in Bruthen flooded back.

"We all have bad dreams, and if you tramp around the bush by yourself for long enough, you're bound to have visions," Joe said. "I've spent many a day in the bush alone, and yes, I've had my share of strange visions, but it's only your mind playing tricks—nothing more."

Bill sat on a rock and looked at his brother.

"Yes, you're probably right, Joe," he said slowly. "Maybe I've been working too hard lately and not getting enough sleep, and my mind's got the better of me."

"I'm bloody certain of it," Joe barked. "Ghosts and visions—it's all rubbish. Forget about it and focus on family and work. You're making good money. You have a lovely family that needs your support. You owe them that. Leave running around after spooks to crackpots who haven't got anything else to do with their miserable lives."

They walked home in silence. The baker was despondent but realised he was becoming preoccupied with his dreams and visions and trying to interpret them. He was not spending enough time with Sarah and the girls, and the thought that he might lose them again hit him hard. He decided then and there to drop his investigation into what his overwrought brain was telling him was a mystery he had to solve. He fumbled in his pocket and found the cigarette butt he'd found in the cave and flicked it into a creek. Good riddance—he had no use for it.

While the baker occasionally ruminated over the cave and his dreams, he didn't go back there and stuck to his baking and family. Anyway, he was looking forward to the weekend tennis competition—the team from Bruthen was coming to play, and of course, old friends like Hodges and Mrs Erskine would be there as well. Saturday was a clear, hot day, and towards noon, the bus from Bruthen arrived along with the tennis team and supporters with picnic lunches. Hodges was first off and raced over to shake the baker's hand, talking at a hundred miles an hour. Mrs Erskine and her husband, Edgar, carrying a large basket, soon appeared. Edgar slowly sauntered over to the baker and Hodges, a huge smirk on his face, while Mrs Erskine, tight-faced and rigid, went to powder her nose. Edgar explained she was still in a huff because of the gags Hodges had told on the bus trip.

"That's just the way she is," he said matter-of-factly.

Hodges kept looking at the ground, trying not to laugh, but happy that he'd got under Mrs Erskine's skin.

The tennis matches were soon underway, but they were of secondary importance to the folks from both towns who had formed into small groups to share their food, and more importantly, gossip and war news. They made their tea from a billy that was simmering on a fire near the pavilion. A group of men had assembled near the fire, and even on this hot day, they stood with their backs to the low flames as if warming themselves. Their talk was only about the war. They wanted to know if the baker had heard anything about his brother, who was a prisoner of war. He said all the family knew was that he was being held somewhere in Italy and apparently receiving reasonable treatment.

Understandably, the war cast a sombre mood over the gathering. It was not going well, with the Japanese advance seemingly unstoppable. Most people believed a Japanese invasion of Australia was inevitable.

The baker left the group to talk with Mrs Erskine and Edgar. The fall of Singapore had rattled her: it was supposed to be impregnable. Edgar comforted his wife, telling her not to worry, and the baker could see Mrs Erskine had been badly affected by the defeat. Singapore was a symbol of the strength of the British Empire and close to Australia. But Mrs Erskine was quick to point out that India was still holding, and she hoped Burma would be retaken, but everyone was gloomy about the likelihood. Still, it was a beautiful day, and she and Edgar had planned a short tour of the caves—informally, with one of the local chaps who knew his way around.

As the baker headed over to Sarah and the kids to get a sandwich and cup of tea, he noticed that Hodges had gone off by himself past the tennis courts and well away from the picnic group. The baker altered course to see if Hodges was alright, and as he approached him, he could see his jovial nature had disappeared and he had a serious, anxious expression on his face. Hodges started by making some small talk about how business in his bakery in Bruthen was going along well enough, and his nephew was picking up the baking trade gradually, which was a relief. Then there was a silence and it seemed Hodges was summoning up the courage to say something to the baker. It came with a rush.

"Look, Bill—some things should be just left alone. No good will come from prying into places that are none of your concern," he said, looking straight into the baker's eyes.

Bill was surprised and not sure what Hodges meant.

"Inexperienced folk like you exploring caves is simply asking for trouble," Hodges quickly added.

"Have you been talking to Joe?" Bill snapped, wondering how Hodges knew about his exploring.

"Don't worry who I've been talking to, but for your own safety's sake, listen to what I'm telling you and stop exploring caves," Hodges growled. "Just stick to marking your ordinance maps with defensive positions and such."

The two men stood in silence facing one another, and Hodges started up again.

"Bill, things that happened in the past are best left in the past. There is no use trying to bring them to light," he advised quietly.

Hodges was becoming increasingly agitated as he talked to his old friend.

"Stop mucking around in the caves and stick with your baking business and enjoying your family," he pleaded.

Then Hodges, looking at the ground, mumbled something about having to umpire a tennis match, but gave one last imploring glance at the baker before he walked back to the courts.

After a short time, the baker wandered back to the picnic area, trying to work out the meaning of Hodges' talk. He wondered how he knew he'd been exploring the caves reserve. Who had told him? As he sat down with Sarah and the kids, she handed him a mutton and pickle sandwich and asked what Hodges had to say.

"Oh, just talking about the baking business and how the war was affecting supplies," he said distractedly, still thinking about Hodges' advice. He didn't want to worry Sarah and, of course, hadn't told her about his exploration of the cave.

He recalled his talk with Joe, who was urging him to give up trying to make sense of his dreams and visions. And now his good mate, Hodges, was saying the same thing. They were his best friends, and both were saying to back off and focus on family and business.

He remembered the terrible time his family endured at Bruthen, having terrifying dreams about the doctor, and he didn't want a repeat of it. As he did after Joe scolded him, the baker acknowledged that Hodges was right; this riddle, if there really was one, was best left alone. He looked at his family enjoying their lunch in the warm sun and glanced over at an animated Hodges arguing over some ruling he'd just given as an umpire. His cave exploring days were over and done.

When the tennis day came to an end, he sought out Hodges and patted him on the back and gave a nod—no more exploring. Hodges understood but said nothing and smiled knowingly.

As the visitor bus departed to Bruthen, the baker noticed Hodges give a thumbs up to George Davies, the farmer who'd been looking at him so intensely at the militia gatherings. With a deep breath, the baker quickly dismissed it and likewise quietened his curiosity.

The Japanese advance continued. They were winning in the Philippines, but worst of all, they had landed in New Guinea. The baker, like everyone else, thought Northern Australia would be next, and God only knows what would happen from there. Still, life went on, and the baker kept working away as best he could with limited supplies. And while the radio brought only bad news, his dreams at least were calm and of little consequence. His duties for the militia now focussed on defensive manoeuvres with the other men. At his request, mapmaking was reallocated to an old bushie who knew the Buchan area better than anyone. He did solve one riddle, though. Old Smithy, who had a piggery just outside town, was buying some bread and casually mentioned it was good to see Hodges and George Davies at the picnic—*cousins*, he thought. And Hodges was godfather to Davies' son, who'd suddenly left home and gone farming in Queensland. The baker let it go at that, but it did lodge in some deep recess of his memory.

Loading up a carrier's truck with bread, the baker joined the driver and headed off to the Lake Tyers Aboriginal Reserve on the coast. He had been awarded a government contract to supply bread twice a week to the Aboriginals, who'd been moved to the reserve. He needed to check with the superintendent that the supplies were going alright and, most importantly, when some payments would be received. Anyway, some fresh sea air would do him good.

There were few people to be seen at the Aboriginal reserve when he arrived, and after dropping off the bread and chatting with the superintendent, he strolled down the road leading to the lake. He spotted an elderly man, white-haired and slimly built, sitting under a tree near a wood pile.

"G'day, mate—how's it going?" he said, smiling at the old man.

The old man smiled back. "Yes, good, mate. Hey, would you like me to make you a boomerang? Maybe you've got kids who'd like it. Only cost a shilling."

The baker agreed, and the old man went to the wood pile, selected a piece of wood, and commenced shaping it with a sharp hatchet. The baker sat on a tree stump, watching closely as the old man crafted the weapon, and he suddenly recalled the white painted Aboriginal he'd seen fleetingly in the caves reserve pointing to the cave entrance he'd explored with his brother.

"Mate, are your people still going to the Buchan caves area for ceremonies—painting themselves with white streaks?" the baker tentatively asked the old man. "I thought I caught sight of a blackfella the other day—painted, like."

The old man said nothing, but he raised his eyes to look at the baker and then finished his carving. He took the boomerang to the campfire and picked up a piece of hot metal wire from the embers, and proceeded to burn letters into the wood, writing "Lake Tyers."

The baker paid his one shilling and took the boomerang, then started to walk back to the truck for the trip home.

The old man suddenly called out to stop and walked over to him. "What did that blackfella look like that you saw?" he asked slowly.

The baker thought for a moment.

"He was a tall, thin man with long black hair. And he was wearing a loincloth and had an animal skin draped over his shoulders. He was pointing to something or somewhere, but I only saw him for a few seconds before he disappeared," the baker said, doing his best to recall the details.

The old man nodded slowly and looked away from the baker.

"That fella you seen was a powerful spirit and he was trying to tell you something. Maybe he wanted to tell you something about blackfellas. Maybe something bad has happened to blackfellas—killed even. That happened plenty of times years ago, even the last few years, in these parts," he said.

Then the old man walked off, but he looked back once more at the baker and yelled in a loud and piercing voice that he should take notice of what he'd seen.

On the drive home, the baker thought about the old man's advice. Like everyone in Gippsland, he'd heard tell of the early settlers shooting Aboriginals, sometimes whole families. He had even heard, on the quiet, that some of the pioneers of Gippsland had carried out organised raids on Aboriginal camps, shooting everyone in sight. But all this happened eighty or more years ago—nothing like that was happening now. And for some reason, the baker thought about the little Irish priest he knew in Bruthen, and it seemed that, once again, this mysterious priest was trying to get him involved in some mystery. But the baker quickly dismissed the thought and started to snooze—he was not getting involved in that world again.

The Japanese were holding their ground in Burma and strengthening their positions in New Guinea. In Europe, Hitler's troops were marching into Russia; the Crimea was under attack, and they were heading to Sebastopol, according to the radio. The baker seriously focussed on his duties with the local militia. It was all he could do to help defend his country. But it was also a break from the bakehouse, and he enjoyed the company of the other blokes. And most importantly, it took his mind off his dreams and signs that some mysterious tragedy may have occurred.

Morale was high in the militia, and even though they were woefully underequipped, there was good comradeship and even a strong belief they could put up a reasonable fight against the Japs.

But try as he might, the baker could not make a friend of George Davies. Neither could any of the other men. Davies kept to himself during the training drills. He was one of the best shots, and that alone singled him out as a valuable member of the militia. He didn't exert himself much or participate in the running drills, but most of the fellows found them difficult. And every couple of minutes, he let out a deep chesty cough, and when he could, he lit a cigarette, taking a deep drag and breathing out the smoke smoothly through his nose and mouth at the same time. He was pretty much left to himself, but the baker sensed that all the time he was watching out for something, and often Davies' eyes drifted towards him.

Darkness fell over the bushland as the militia finished off training one evening, and the baker found himself walking alone with Davies on the path back to the meeting hall. As usual, Davies was smoking, and he offered the baker a cigarette, which he gladly accepted. The baker made some small talk about the war going badly, and Davies grunted something about it probably getting worse. Then Davies stopped, and the baker sensed he wanted to say something to him. He didn't say much; only, he looked away in the distance and said the baker would be well advised to take Hodges' advice and keep away from exploring caves, because… well… it was dangerous. He looked at the baker to see whether he understood, and while the baker silently nodded affirmation, he also understood there was a lot more to this story. He had resisted the temptation, but now he again began thinking it was his job to get to the bottom of it.

The two men walked on, and Davies asked about the baker's brother, Joe. He was reputedly the best shot in Gippsland, and the baker confirmed that Joe had no peer—he didn't even bother holding the rifle to his shoulder these days but shot rabbits from the hip. Davies nodded his admiration, then said Joe would have no trouble hitting any invading Japanese soldiers. He stared again into the distance and remarked that a man is a big target when you shoot for the torso. The baker wondered what he was talking about, but then they arrived at the hall and broke company.

The baker snatched a couple of hours sleep before his night's baking, feeling replete after a meal of rissoles and vegetables Sarah had cooked. The family was settled and content, and he didn't want to do anything to break the harmony, but this mystery involving Davies dominated his mind even more than the war news. As he lay under the covers, he knew he had pieces of the jigsaw, but their meaning eluded him entirely. He relaxed, and his breathing became deep and regular and suddenly he was in the bush surrounded by fog or smoke, and he could hear falling water. Then hazy, undefined human shapes appeared—a man and a woman—and they had a child with them, but there was another person there, too; someone very much alone and afraid, who set themselves apart from the others like someone who doesn't belong. And then, the statue like figure of the Aboriginal pointing to some place appeared; its gestures were strong and emphatic. Finally, a shadow spread over the whole scene—the unmistakable silhouette of the Irish priest the baker knew in Bruthen. The baker woke up gradually, and sharp consciousness returned. He was soaked in sweat, his mind racing and confused. Terror gripped his heart. As he recovered his composure and found his bearings, he knew that, despite the warnings of Davies and Hodges, he should again return to the cave he had started to explore with Joe. But at the same instant, a strong feeling arose: *Just leave it alone, forget about it, just look to the welfare of your own family*. He dragged himself out of bed and prepared for a night's baking.

When he'd finished his baking early the next morning, he went into the house to make a cup of tea and some toast before Sarah and the kids began stirring. He was surprised to find them slumped around the kitchen table, silent and looking tired.

"I didn't expect to see a welcoming committee this early," he joked.

Sarah looked up. A forced smile creased her face before she stretched her mouth into a huge yawn and rubbed her eyes.

"Seems like we've had a night of dreams—and strange dreams at that," she said wearily. "The only one not dreaming was the baby, and she didn't have a very settled night."

Helen and Ruthie were virtually asleep sitting up, but their faces brightened when their father gave them a cuddle.

"Tell Dad about your dream, love," Sarah said to Helen.

"I was walking along the path near the swimming pool in the reserve, and suddenly, I fell over," Helen said slowly, trying to recall every detail of the dream. "When I tried to stand up, I fell over again. And when I looked behind me, there was this minister—he looked like that priest at the Catholic church down the road, but he was smaller and bald. I think he was making me fall over, but he didn't say anything—he just looked at me like he was angry."

"Ruthie had the same dream," Sarah said, looking toward her daughter, who nodded in agreement. "And as for me, I dreamt I fell off the bridge leading into the reserve. I called out for help, but nobody came to my assistance. But some Catholic priest, like the one Helen dreamt about, was looking over the side of the bridge, and he didn't look like he would help me."

The baker sat down heavily in a kitchen chair—the dreams of his family had come as a shock.

"What's all this about, Bill?" Sarah asked, expecting him to come up with a ready answer.

But the baker just shook his head, indicating he had no idea. He was afraid Sarah might ask about his dreams, but she didn't and instead went to a place Bill feared.

"It feels like we're back in Bruthen years ago when we all had nightmares about the doctor and those frightening noises were coming out of the laboratory," she said tensely. "Tell me it's not happening again, Bill. I couldn't go through that again, neither could the girls."

"That's not going to happen," Bill quickly responded. "It's just a night of bad dreams. It's not as if you're dreaming this dream night after night—it was only last night, wasn't it?"

Sarah conceded it was the only night she'd had the dream, and Helen and Ruthie agreed.

"And there are no strange noises, so it's not like Bruthen at all," Bill said, trying to reassure everyone while feeling nausea arising within himself and every muscle in his back and neck tense up. "You'll see. This is just an odd night. Everything will be back to normal in no time."

Sarah climbed wearily from her chair and started to prepare breakfast. She was only partially reassured by Bill's words, and she could see Helen and Ruthie had their doubts. Anyway, she was too tired to argue, and maybe Bill was right—it would soon pass, particularly after a good night's sleep.

Sarah and the girls returned to bed for a snooze after breakfast, but Bill remained at the kitchen table, tense and a feeling of anger arising within him.

So that's how that bloody priest plays it, he thought. *If I decide not to do his bidding, he goes to work on my family, giving them bad dreams and terrifying them. All just to get back at me. He's holding me to ransom: "Do what I want, or you lose your family – that's his game."*

He mulled it over, this way and that, but there was only one way out—he had to go back to the cave and find out what secrets it held.

A few days later, he headed back to the cave, this time well equipped for exploring with a stout, long rope, a strong hurricane lantern, proper leather boots, and a bag of tools. Nearing the falls, he heard the resonant pounding of the water as he secured his rope around the trunk of a tree before entering the cave. Fixing a lantern to the rope to light his way, he descended into the darkness of the rock shaft that oozed a slimy green dampness. Passing his previous mark and with trembling legs, he groped his way downwards, finally settling his boots on a firm footing. He cast his light around and saw that he stood in a large, moist cavern dripping with water. Tiny white stalactites eerily adorned the roof. It was a fair size, and he loosened himself from the rope and steadily plodded around, trying to avoid slipping on the wet rock floor. It was deathly quiet aside from the regular high-pitched drumming of water dripping from the roof. But there was nothing much to see—it was just a large rock cavern—still and foreboding in its way, but featureless.

The baker made his way to the far end of the cavern and saw a hole, much narrower than the entrance, dropping downwards to an unknown depth. Then his foot suddenly touched against something, and it moved, falling into the abyss on whose edge he stood. He listened to hear when it hit the bottom and, after a few seconds, heard a faint thud. He instinctively moved away from the hole—there would be no escape if he fell into it. But then a rock shelf nearby caught his attention, and he slowly scrambled over to examine it. And when he held his lantern higher, he made out a layer of rough hessian cloth that had been placed at the back of the ledge. He paused because he knew in himself that whatever lay under the covering was the reason he had mysteriously been directed to the cave, and his thoughts returned to finding the mummified skeletal remains of the Lambert brothers in his father's old mine at Deptford a few years earlier. He had the support of the priest then, but this time he was alone. His breathing settled, though, becoming deep and rhythmic. A calm strength descended on him as he knew the hessian cover needed to be removed to reveal its contents. He grasped the edge of the rough cloth and gently raising it and pulling it aside, knowing in his heart and mind what would be revealed, and sure enough, skeletal remains covered in ragged clothing appeared, chalky white before him—the skulls with their familiar macabre toothy grins. The baker recoiled and sat in shock on the damp floor of the cave.

His mind racing, the baker was incredulous. Why was this happening to him—again? The experience of finding the Lamberts with a priest who was apparently some type of ghost was more than enough for any man, yet here it was happening again, and God knows what the story was as to how these remains got here. With the guidance of the priest, he'd managed to untangle the story behind the Lamberts' demise, but this time, there seemed little to go on, and in any case, the baker did not feel up to solving another mystery and resented finding himself in this situation. He should have listened to Joe and Hodges and stayed out of it, minding his own business, but the dreams his family experienced pushed him to act.

But here he was, and that part of him, curious and compassionate, finally asserted itself. There was no shirking what had to be done—solve the mystery of the remains and, in some way, undo a knot in the natural order of the universe. So, he slowly stood, the seat of his pants saturated from sitting on the wet rock floor, and once again, he prepared himself to examine skeletal remains.

Holding up the lantern, he cast its light over the skeletons. They were arranged oddly. Two adults lay together with a clump of cloth between them. A third skeleton was placed well apart from the other two, and its clothing seemed in better condition. And it appeared to have been set in position correctly, its arms by its sides and legs together. The other two seemed to have been thrown down haphazardly—the arms and legs askew. The baker scrambled up on the ledge to take a closer look at the two skeletons closest together. The remains of their clothing looked like thin, cheap material, and it was mostly decayed. But the clump of cloth between the two caught the baker's attention, and as he gently lifted it, he was horrified to find a small skeleton, obviously that of a child. It was clothed in the same fabric as the others, and the cloth had all but rotted away. The baker quickly retreated from the ledge and stood still, trying to understand his discovery. Questions raced through his mind: what were the identities of these dead people? How had they come to be here? Had they been trapped, unable to escape? But looming large in his mind was the question: what should he do now?

He'd had enough of the cave and, securing his lantern and tools, went back to the rope to climb out. His eyes caught sight of some small white objects on the floor, and it was no surprise when he recognised them as cigarette butts—the same type as he'd seen previously. They were fresh with no signs of dust or discolouration. Someone had been here recently. With considerable effort, the baker scrambled hand over hand up the rope, getting some purchase with his boots, and finally crawled towards the welcome daylight of the cave entrance, his muscles screaming with fatigue. He looked around the surrounding bush, half expecting to see someone watching him, but he was alone, and with the light fading fast, he walked home, sullen and thoughtful, to figure out his next move.

In the bakery that night, he considered his options. The obvious thing to do was tell the police and let them solve the mystery of the skeletons. But welling up within him was another feeling, and it became stronger the longer he thought about the situation: don't tell anyone about what he'd seen and just let it all play out. He sat on an old wooden chair, ruminating on the proper course to follow, and his thoughts went back to the time he'd found the bodies of the Lamberts in his father's old mine at Mount Welcome. He had a wise and trusted adviser then— the Catholic priest—and the baker recalled him saying that police and officials have no place in some affairs; justice is best found by taking matters into your own hands. But the baker was torn by his decision not to tell the police: it seemed the right and proper course of action. He passed the night, pulled this way and that by his internal conflict, but finally resolved to let it rest for a week, maybe two, and see what turned up. He felt relief with his decision, drawing in deep, calming breaths, and his mind was resolute—wait a little longer.

While the baker chose to wait, someone else had decided to make their presence known. Late one morning, the baker discovered a small pane of glass in the bakery window had been broken, perhaps by someone trying to rob the place. But when he checked inside, nothing had been taken or moved out of place. Then, the top of the letterbox was wrenched off and left lying on the ground. The baker thought someone was trying to give him a message rather than steal anything. Maybe it was a message to mind his own business, delivered by someone unknown. The perplexed baker decided to stick to his guns and just wait it out—he was sure something would happen soon that would solve the mystery. But he wasn't expecting sudden misfortune.

He was setting off to deliver bread on his cart one morning when his horse stopped in its tracks, started lurching from side to side, then, with a huge thud, fell dead onto the road, almost overturning the cart. The baker jumped down out of fright and saw the horse was no longer breathing. He looked around hurriedly, perhaps expecting someone to be watching, but there was no one. Presently, townsfolk and store owners came to his assistance, but as the cart was unhitched with difficulty from the prostrate horse, the baker wondered if foul play was involved—foul play that was unwarranted, but by whom?

The baker's daughters were horrified by the horse carcass, and he had to walk them to school on the opposite side of the road while, all the time, they trembled and averted their eyes. It was the local farmer, George Davies, from the militia, who showed up a day later to remove the dead creature. He quickly winched the carcass onto a low cart and secured it, all the while staying silent as the baker watched.

When he'd finished, he glanced over at the baker's letterbox.

"That needs fixing," he said. "Want me to do it?"

The baker told him he would repair it.

"Alright, at least I offered," he said with a shrug. "I'll get rid of the carcass at no cost. Hey, I even know a bloke who can sell you a good cart horse, cheap. I'll bring it over if you like. After all, we don't want your business to suffer and people to go without bread." Davies smirked as he leaned against his cart, lighting a cigarette.

The baker suspected Davies was somehow behind all this, but he had no proof. He felt a sudden surge of anger and wanted to grab Davies by the throat and find out what the hell he was playing at but managed to keep control.

"I'll take you up on that offer on the horse," he said quietly. "Would you arrange for it to be brought over?"

Then, through gritted teeth, he thanked Davies and headed back to the bakery. He watched as the still smirking Davies drove his cart out of town.

No doubt he thinks he's delivered me a message to leave everything well enough alone, he thought to himself. *Yes, somehow, Davies is the key to this mystery.*

The weather was closing in as the baker walked to the bakery for his night's work. The easterly wind blew dark clouds across the moonless sky. Heavy rain was in the offing and plenty of it. News of the war on the radio was still bleak, but at least the Japanese hadn't landed in Australia. He thought about his brother, Cyril, in the POW camp in Italy and wondered how he was getting on, reassuring himself that Cyril was a tough young bloke who could handle himself pretty well.

The baker tried to reason with himself that he had bigger concerns than those he'd found in the cave, but it was no use—the mystery of the cave was gnawing at him day and night, and right now, he was doing nothing to solve it, nor seeing any way of doing so. Maybe it was time to go to the police.

Davies was good to his word and brought the horse to the baker next day. It was a strong beast, ideal for cart work, and seemed to have a good temperament. The price was reasonable, so the baker paid in cash and thanked Davies for arranging it.

"We all have to help one another, particularly during these difficult times," Davies said pointedly.

"Yes, I can't disagree with that," the baker responded, all the time thinking that Davies was not only talking about the horse but something else as well.

As they finished their conversation, Davies turned to go, but suddenly started coughing deeply and grasped a fence post to steady himself. The coughing attack lasted about ten seconds, and the baker asked if he was alright—did he need some water? But Davies waved him away mumbling that he was fine as he wiped his mouth with his handkerchief—just that something must have gone down the wrong way. The baker watched as he walked unsteadily to his cart and slowly drove out of town.

He turned to go back into the bakery but suddenly caught sight of two Aboriginals sitting under a tree just across the road. One was the old man who had made him the boomerang at Lake Tyers, and he was accompanied by an equally old, white-haired woman. And out of the corner of his eye, the baker noticed that Davies had stopped his cart some distance away and was looking back towards the bakery.

The baker walked towards the Aboriginal as it seemed they wanted to talk to him, but not while Davies, still watching from afar, was hanging around. They waved the baker away and waited in the trees until Davies' cart was finally out of sight. Only then did the Aboriginals approach the baker.

"Did your kids like the boomerang I made them?" the old man said, but the woman cut him off.

"Tell me about the blackfella spirit you saw," she implored the baker.

The baker didn't let on exactly where he had seen the figure but gave a fair description, particularly the fact that it was pointing out something to him.

By now the woman was crying and had her hands to her face, softly wailing to herself, and the old man next to her stared fixedly at the ground, mumbling that something was "no bloody good."

"My son and his wife and their little fella are missing," the woman suddenly screamed out. "Couple of years ago, they went out walking to see uncles and aunties but never came back home like they should. Something bad must have happened to them."

She put her head in her hands and wept and moaned uncontrollably, and the old man tried to comfort her as best he could.

The old man looked squarely at the baker. "You have to help us," he pleaded. "You've been visited by the spirit, and he knows the truth about things."

But the baker dismissed their appeal, but he knew the skeletons in the cave were the remains of the missing family.

"I don't know anything about any missing blackfellas. Maybe they've gone to some other place where their relatives live," he said.

The two elderly Aboriginals moved closer and once again begged for the baker's help, but he was adamant he couldn't assist them.

Eventually, they wandered off, the woman still sobbing while the old man looked back imploringly at the baker. And in the far distance, Davies making his way home on his cart was just a speck on the horizon.

That night, the baker had a tough time baking anything. His thoughts were overwhelming him, and his stomach heaved—he was almost breathless, brought on no doubt by the guilt of not being honest with the Aboriginals who had sought his help. Why he clammed up about the skeletons in the cave was beyond him; only something stopped him from saying anything—God knows what. He threw the dough he was kneading back onto the workbench and sat at his table, tired and more confused than ever. There was no priest to advise him this time on how he should proceed, and he felt his loneliness acutely. For some reason, his thoughts turned to Psalm 23 and the line that went "for Thou art with me," but it provided little of the reassurance and comfort he longed for. The baker was at his wit's end—it was time to put the matter into someone else's hands. He resolved to go to the police next morning and let them take care of the mystery.

He wearily rose to return to work, but suddenly, the bakehouse door swung open with a bang, and George Davies strode in, shotgun in hand, his wild eyes glaring at the baker. Slamming the door behind him, he menacingly motioned the baker back to his seat with the gun.

"You just don't listen, do you?" growled Davies as he sat in a chair, resting the gun on the table, the barrel pointed straight at the baker. "You keep sticking your nose in where it's not wanted, stirring things up that are best left alone."

The dumbfounded baker looked at the gun and pleaded that he had no idea what Davies was talking about, but Davies quickly cut him off. "You know what I mean," he said. "You've been poking about in the cave down near the falls, and you know what's in there. And you've been talking to them Aboriginals, right? What the hell did you tell them?"

The baker was silent for a few seconds and, trying not to upset Davies any more than he was, agreed with him. "Yes, alright, I've seen the remains in the cave and talked with the Aboriginals, but I didn't tell them about the cave. Look, I haven't got any idea what any of this means and what it's got to do with you," he said.

Davies studied the baker momentarily, then growled, "Who the hell have you told about this—the cave and what's in it, I mean?"

The baker shook his head and replied "No one—not a soul, and that's the truth," he said.

"Is that right?" Davies mocked. "And why haven't you run to the police? You must have told your wife and brother."

"Listen," the baker said firmly. "I haven't told anyone, and that's because I've seen this type of thing before, and I wanted to wait to see what came of it, and sure enough, with you coming here tonight, the pieces are falling into place."

Davies screwed up his face in disbelief at what the baker was telling him. He was totally bamboozled.

"What do you mean you've seen it before?" he snarled.

"It's a long story" the baker replied. "Let's just say that police and courts and officials don't always understand what's really happening some of the time, let alone dispense justice."

"You got that right," Davies snapped. "I've never had any time for police or judges. But a bloke like you—seems to me you're one for doing things properly, according to the law."

"I'm not debating that now," the baker said. "I'm wondering what all this is about?"

Davies sat quietly, sizing up the baker. He lit a cigarette and took a deep drag, then wisps of smoke slowly issued forth from his mouth and nostrils for a good ten seconds.

"There's a story behind it all right: a story that should be over and done with, except you chose to drag it all up with your poking about, not listening when you should have," Davies said bitterly. "But where do we go from here? I don't know. It's up to you, really," he added grimly.

He cast a threatening glance at the baker. He meant to get his way, but he wasn't sure how.

The baker said he had to cover his bread dough and moved to stand up, but Davies laid his hand on the shotgun and motioned the baker to resume his seat.

Then Davies suddenly sprang to his feet.

"You're the problem here, you and your bloody curiosity. Sticking your nose in where it's not wanted," he said in an accusatory tone. He pointed his finger at the baker and was about to continue his verbal assault when a deep cough burst out of his throat, followed by a deeper hoarse tremor as his face turned crimson red and he struggled for breath. Davies bent over, propping himself unsteadily on the table, still coughing deeply and trying to get his breath when a bloody sputum rocketed out of his mouth, splashing onto the floor. He dropped back, exhausted and breathless, into his chair and seemed at the point of passing out.

The baker seized his opportunity and grabbed the shotgun, quickly unloading it and throwing the cartridges out a window into the dark garden behind the bakery. He threw the gun into the storeroom, which he locked, and then returned to find Davies still struggling for breath but conscious and regaining his composure. The baker took up a clean piece of rag and handed it to Davies, who mopped his mouth, leaving blotches of blood on the cloth. He sat calmly now that the attack was over, slowly wiping his mouth, dejected and defeated.

The baker placed a glass of water on the table then resumed his seat, waiting for Davies to recover enough to talk.

"All right, what's this all about, George?" said the baker. "It's high time the truth came out."

Davies took his time, breathing slowly with the odd cough, which he relieved with sips of water. "The truth?" he said sarcastically. "Yes, all right, I'll give you the honest truth—it doesn't matter anymore because I'm rooted." He stared vacantly at the bakery wall, collecting his thoughts. "It's cancer, they tell me; in the lungs and chest, probably all through me." Davies sneered. "Not that I care; death will be a bloody relief after what I've been through and living in a body that's shot."

The baker asked how long he had left. Davies said it was only a matter of months, if that.

But the baker pressed on, demanding Davies tell him about the cave and the remains it held. Still weakened and sometimes gasping for breath, Davies told his story.

"It all started a couple of years ago when me and my son were out shooting on the property."

The baker interrupted and asked if he was talking about his son, who'd gone farming in Queensland.

"Just listen!" Davies insisted. "Yes, Jim and me, we were out shooting wild dogs, and we come across a dead sheep—freshly killed with its hind quarters cut away. We'd been losing the odd sheep on the property, and I put it down to the dogs. But Jim reckoned someone was killing the sheep. Anyway, we saw smoke rising from near the creek and crept over and knelt behind a big red gum to see what was going on. That's when we saw a group of blackfellas - a man about the same age as Jim and a woman nursing a child. They were sitting around a fire cooking meat - no doubt the sheep they'd just killed. And, before I knew it, Jim had taken aim at the blacks, and his first shot brought down the woman. And then a second shot that hit the kid. I spun around and pushed up the barrel of his rifle and told him to stop, but he cursed and said the blacks were nothing but thieves and deserved what they'd just got. The black man took flight into the bush, and all I could see was the lifeless bodies of the woman and child lying on the ground near the fire."

Davies stared blankly at the table. "Jim and me, with our rifles ready, walked over to the fire to where the bodies lay,'" he said. "The woman had been shot through the chest, and the child had a deep head wound. Both were dead. The woman's eyes were still open, and there was a look of horror on her face. I cursed Jim and asked why the bloody hell he'd opened fire, and by now, he saw the brutality of his actions, and he just stood there, white-faced and mute. Then, suddenly, something hit him in the head—a large rock—and he fell to the ground, unconscious. I quickly looked to see who'd thrown the rock and saw the black man standing near a bush some ten yards off. Instinctively, I put my gun to my shoulder and fired two rounds in quick succession. The blackfella dropped where he stood; I'd hit him in the heart twice, and he was dead. I just stood there as the echo of my last shots faded, surrounded by four bodies. When I checked Jim, he wasn't breathing. Blood was running out of his nose and mouth—his body was limp, and I couldn't find a pulse. I was numb with shock, trying to fathom how such an awful tragedy could take place, almost in the blink of an eye."

The baker had been silent while Davies told his story, and now ventured to suggest the outcome of the shooting.

"So, you took matters into your own hands, and rather than telling the police what happened, you moved the bodies into the cave and put about the story your son had upped and gone to Queensland to take up farming."

"Yes, that's about it," said Davies. "His mother was inconsolable, but she took comfort from the fact he wouldn't be remembered as a murderer and went along with what I'd done. But I promised her that one day, I'd arrange a proper burial for him. God knows how. Anyway, that's the story."

Davies sat quietly, exhausted, wracked by his illness, gasping for breath, yet relieved his burden had been lifted by confessing the truth of his actions. The baker leant back in his chair, considering all he'd heard, knowing that somehow it had fallen to him to bring an end to this tragedy. He knew some unseen hand had been directing him to resolve this whole mess right from the time he'd seen the cave in the dusk and the Aboriginal spirit pointing it out and through his dreams. And he knew that a practical solution like going to the police was not in order— justice had to be found through other means.

He turned it over in his mind for a minute, then turned to Davies.

"All right, here's what we'll do," he said in quiet conspiratorial tones. "We must move the bodies from the cave and arrange decent burials for them. Don't worry—there's no need to get undertakers or anyone else involved; we can do it ourselves. We have to put an end to this and get the remains of the Aboriginals back to their people. As for your son, you'll have to decide what you want done with his remains."

Davies was sceptical. "Them blackfellas will go to the police once they're given the remains, that's for sure," he said. "And then the whole story will come out, and the police will be on to me and my family. I don't care a fig what they do to me, but I don't want them hounding my wife. As for Jim—yes, he should be buried right and proper."

The baker saw things differently. "The blackfellas won't go to the police because they don't trust them, or any of us white folk, for that matter. It's no wonder after what the early settlers around these parts are reputed to have done to them. No, they just want the remains back so they can perform the proper burial rites. I'm sure of it," he said.

"They can come after me if they want," said Davies. "It doesn't matter now. Just as long as they leave my wife in peace."

"There'll be no revenge on your wife," said the baker. "I'll see to that. As for you, you'll have to take your chances, but nobody will hear from me what you've done."

The two men sat quietly for a while. Then Davies suddenly broke down, sobbing while trying to get his breath.

"God, I never meant it to happen. I don't know what got into Jim's head. How he could shoot a woman and child," he moaned. "But Jim was never right in the head since that doctor treated him when he was a kid."

"What doctor?" the baker asked.

"The one in Bruthen—I've forgotten his name, but he was a bloody crackpot," Davies said.

"Doctor Crawford, do you mean?' the baker asked.

"Yes, that's him," Davies said, with a sneer. "Jim was just a young fella, and he came down with flu or something. Everyone said take him to the doctor in Bruthen—he's an expert. So, we did, and the doctor injected him with some medicine he'd prepared. But Jim passed out and there was no rousing him. We took him straight home, and he was semi-conscious for a week. And when he fully woke up, he wasn't the same—he was slow and dopey, and he stayed that way. He'd been sharp as a tack before the doctor messed him up.

Another victim of Doctor Crawford, the baker thought angrily. *And that's why the priest has got me involved in this mess—undoing the doctor's mistakes again.*

The baker took stock of the situation and turned to Davies.

"It's a bad business, alright," he said. "But all we can do now is clean it up as best we can."

Davies nodded agreement, then looked at the baker, seeking his help.

"Look, Bill, we've never been friends, but right now, I need you to be the best friend I've ever had. I trust you to square things away with the blackfellas, but I want Jim to be laid to rest properly. I know I'm buggered; it's only a matter of time before I kick off. Maybe we could arrange it in some way that Jim and me end up in the same grave," he said.

The baker smiled grimly. "Strange you should mention it, but that's just what I had in mind. But I'll need your help to retrieve the remains from the cave. Are you up to it?" he said.

"Sure," said Davies. "But you'll have to do the lion's share—I just haven't got the strength."

"That's fine," said the baker. "Now take yourself home and get some rest. I'll set it all up and be in contact shortly."

Davies lurched to his feet, balancing himself on the table. The baker could see his days were numbered, so he would have to move quickly. He watched as Davies, perched on his horse-drawn cart, disappeared into the night, then quickly got back to baking and planning his next move.

The baker listened to the midday news on the radio. The war was grinding on with the Japanese trying to move through New Guinea, but finally, they were meeting some resistance from the Australian army. And American forces and ships were arriving, and it was now more likely that an invasion of Australia would be averted. He was cautious about the news—there was a lot to be done before the Japanese threat was eliminated. But at least the Russians were in the European war after the German invasion—hopefully, they would put up a decent fight against Hitler.

But his mind was elsewhere. He had hatched out a plan to remove the remains from the cave and sent a message to Davies to meet him there one afternoon during the week when it was unlikely anyone would be around. The baker arrived early, bringing two long, stout ropes and climbing gear along with some canvas bags for the remains. The area around the cave was eerily quiet, and the baker felt uneasy and on edge, sensing that an unnatural presence was nearby. He cast his eyes around the surrounding bushland but saw nothing out of the ordinary. Then Davies appeared on the track, coughing deeply and carrying a large, heavy sack on his shoulders. He laid out the contents—lanterns, canvas sheets and a small winch to help lower and raise the baker and the remains.

After Davies caught his breath, he listened closely for any noises that would indicate other people were nearby, but he heard nothing, only the sound of water from the falls.

"I can't hear anyone, but for the life of me, I could swear someone else is around here," he said warily to the baker.

"Yes, I know what you mean," said the baker, "but I've had a good look around and can't see anyone, so let's get on with it."

Davies quickly set up the winch and attached a folded canvas sheet to hold the remains.

"Listen, you're in no condition to go down there," the baker said. "You operate the winch, and I'll go down and gather everything up."

Davies agreed, and soon the baker was being lowered into the cave with a lantern tied to the rope to light his way. When he reached the bottom, he yelled to Davies to stop lowering and, taking a lantern, cast its light around the cave. All was the same as it was previously, and he inched his way over to the skeletal remains. The flickering shadows in the cave gave the baker the sense he wasn't alone—not by a long shot— yet nothing untoward appeared before him. The baker set to work quickly so he could get out of the place as soon as possible.

One by one, the baker brought the skeletons, still covered in dusty, thin clothing, to the canvas sheet and Davies winched them up at the baker's signal. When all four skeletons had been raised, the baker scrambled up the rope with the assistance of Davies operating the winch. When he reached the top, he saw a distraught Davies sitting on a rock, tears flowing down his cheeks, looking at the remains of his son: the skull cracked open. The baker paused to take in the scene before him: untimely death brought about by the foolishness of a bigoted, hot-tempered man. And he pondered how events, insignificant in themselves, like stealing a sheep, can lead to immense tragedy. But it was high time they left the bush as dusk was starting to descend.

At the baker's urging, Davies helped secure the remains in the canvas bags for the journey back to the cart. Loaded up, the two men started out with Davies leading, but he suddenly dropped to his knees, coughing deeply and with his right arm pointing to something. The baker looked ahead, and there in a clearing stood the figure of an Aboriginal, adorned with white paint, bolt upright, and standing on one leg with the other foot on his inner thigh. There was a long spear in his right hand. He glared as if his eyes were on fire and he looked directly at the kneeling Davies as if to curse him. Davies was transfixed, unmoving, and could not break off from looking at the figure. The Aboriginal was perfectly still but then slowly lifted his spear and pointed it at Davies, and the baker thought he was about to throw it. But instead, the figure slowly moved back into the bush, never for a moment taking its fierce eyes off Davies, nor lowing his spear. And suddenly, it vanished.

The baker steadied the load on the ground and checked Davies, who was white-faced and trembling all over.

"Good God, what was that?" Davies asked the baker in a trembling voice.

The baker knew it was an ill omen but said they should ignore it and get on with the job at hand.

Davies took a few minutes to recover enough to again take up the burden, and he proceeded forward in silence. Now he knew his fate had been sealed.

As they loaded the cart, the baker saw that Davies looked calm, even relaxed, and he wondered what had become of the anguish over his again seeing his son's remains and the appearance of the Aboriginal spectre.

They drove the cart back to the baker's house, and after Bill checked that his family was occupied inside and would not disturb them, the two men deftly moved the bags of remains into a small shed behind the house. Bill locked it and then walked back to the horse and cart to see Davies off home.

"So, what's next?" Davies asked.

The baker had been considering this question but spoke plainly.

"The bags stay put until…"

"Until I die, and then you promise to somehow bury Jim with me?" Davies interjected.

"That's about it," the baker said, nodding.

Davies stretched out his hand and shook the baker's hand.

"I won't be around for long, and the blackfella we just saw confirmed it, I reckon," Davies said. "I'm not scared of dying—I've lived long enough. Maybe now is the time to face up to a higher court for what I've done."

He boarded the cart and cast a glance at the baker.

"I had you all wrong and I'm sorry," he said. "If it wasn't for you, well, I'd be dying with everything not properly squared away, that's for sure. But maybe I can find some peace at last, if there is peace for the likes of me."

The baker again noticed tears in Davies' eyes, and he watched as his cart disappeared from view as he went on his homeward journey.

A few days later, Sarah, after coming back from shopping late one morning, gave the baker the news he'd been expecting.

"You know that farmer, Davies, who sold you the horse?" she said. "Well, Doris at the grocery said he upped and died last night. Apparently, he had cancer all through him. And they're not waiting long for the funeral—it's tomorrow afternoon."

The baker nodded his understanding and even feigned a look of surprise but gave Sarah no indication that anything was out of the ordinary. He immediately started making his plans to bury Davies' son's remains in the grave that no doubt would be dug today. He made ready his pick, spade, and lanterns for the grim task and set them next to the bag of bones—Jim's remains—he had to bury.

Soon after midnight, as the townsfolk slept, he stealthily crept through the dark streets to the cemetery and went to the grave he'd seen being dug yesterday afternoon. He quickly shovelled out enough dirt from the base of the grave, then laid the remains of Jim Davies to rest before covering them with dirt and making everything look as he'd found it.

At one stage, he paused to reflect on his work.

First, it was the Lambert brothers in Bruthen, and now Jim Davies' belated burial, he thought. *Maybe Jim is reunited with his father in death, and maybe not. But if there is a God to whom everyone is accountable, how will Jim explain his cruel actions, and for that matter, how will his father account for his?*

The baker looked towards the heavens. Thankfully, there was no moon tonight, so the darkness would provide good cover for his deed and eventual return to the bakery.

***

While he'd kept his promise to Davies, the baker turned over in his mind how he could get the remains of the Aboriginals back to their family. In his heart, he knew he had to act with complete honesty—that for once, at least, a white man would do the right thing by blackfellas. So, he again hitched a ride to the Lake Tyers settlement on the pretext of talking about bread deliveries with the superintendent, but knowing he had to tell the truth to the relatives of the murdered family somehow.

The baker had a brief talk with the superintendent, but he was not the least bit interested in what the dreary official was saying. Then, he headed off for a walk around the settlement. As he turned behind the back of a small shack towards the wood heap where the boomerang was made, the old man and woman he'd encountered previously sat on a log as if they expected him. They raised their eyes, looking for the baker to provide them with the information they wanted, but not saying a word. The baker stopped short of them and avoided eye contact by looking at the ground. He could hear a soft whimper arising from the old woman and feared she would start wailing.

The old man stood and walked over to the baker.

"Look here, Mr O'Connell. We know they're dead, and we know it was most likely a bad business, but we just want to know where they are—that's most important to us," he said. "Bugger trying to get even or anything—we just want them back."

The baker cleared his throat and raised his head to look at the old man.

"Yes, it was a bad business, alright—it was bloody murder, but not me, you understand—another whitefella and his son. Both of them are dead now, and that's the truth."

The woman moaned, and the old man murmured for her to keep quiet, then asked the baker about the remains and where he could find them.

But the baker pressed the old man as to whether he was going to the police. "No police, no bloody lawmen," the old man snarled. "Whitefella justice is for whitefellas, always has been. Just tell me where they are!"

Bumping along in the truck back to Buchan, the baker felt a sense of disgust arising within him.

How is it that a family can be murdered in cold blood, and what makes people carry out such acts? he thought, realising he had not the faintest hope of answering his own question. *And not even telling the police. There is something very much wrong.*

But at least he had told the old man and woman where the remains of their kin could be found—securely packed away in a large canvas bag in the branches of a big willow tree by the river, just south of town. He would put it there tomorrow, not that he'd said that to the Aboriginals. He just told them the location and to wait a day or two.

———————————

Morose and tired, the baker returned home, went into the kitchen, and plonked down at the table. Sarah made them tea and, seeing her husband was lost in his own thoughts, leafed through the newspaper, reading out some snippets she thought were interesting. But the news was grim: war and death. And she thought how her husband must be worried sick about his brother in the prisoner of war camp in Italy. And she thought how many families were thinking about their loved ones taken away from them by the insanity of violence and war.

Night was falling as the baker went out for a walk after dinner to try to lift his spirits. He just could not settle his nerves and a feeling of impatience that had taken hold of him. There was no one about town, and only the distant bellows of cattle broke the silence. He slowly ambled towards the cemetery, not for any particular reason, but remembered that Davies would have been buried earlier in the day, and so he decided to walk to the grave. As he approached, he could see that fresh earth had been piled into a low mound on top of the grave. In time, a monument would be erected, but it would not bear witness to all the deceased in that grave.

Yet even at this hour, there was a lone mourner still at the grave site—a figure in black and strangely familiar in profile to the baker. As he drew nearer, the figure turned to face him. It was the little Irish priest who had been his adviser in Bruthen—a man who did not exist, but here he was, seemingly large as life. The baker stopped dead in his tracks and looked at the priest's face. It was full of longing and deeply etched with suffering. In his silence, his expression pleaded with the baker to end his suffering. But there was something else the baker felt—a sense of foreboding. The figure of the priest was indistinct, far more so than in Bruthen, where it had been vivid and lifelike. It was as if he was fading away. Then, the figure glided slowly and silently away from the grave and, in a moment, disappeared into the darkness.

The baker knew his work with the priest was far from finished. He knew that somehow he was destined to relieve the suffering of others, not the least being the priest himself. But the priest had given him a dire warning, and the baker ruefully contemplated the challenges and dangers that might lay ahead.

The Baker of Gippsland

Korumburra

1948

The war has ended, but times remain tough. The baker and his family have made a fresh start in the prosperous coal and dairy town of Korumburra in South Gippsland. While the baker laid to rest some ghosts years earlier, unresolved tragedies of long ago will again beckon him to decipher cryptic glues to bring peace to troubled souls, including the mysterious Irish priest.

———————————

Mavis, the shop assistant, had never seen anything like it. She'd only worked at the bakery for two weeks, but why people would suddenly form a queue outside the shop and not come inside was beyond her understanding. There was no one in the shop apart from her. Mystified and a little worried, she called out in a high-pitched, strained voice, "Mr O'Connell, quickly, come and see this."

The baker was standing near the door leading to the bakehouse. He turned around to see what was happening, and a huge grin swept over his face. Mavis was rigid with amazement, staring at the quiet and orderly queue forming outside the shop.

"Good Lord, Mavis, what's going on?" he cried in mock astonishment. "Why don't they come inside?"

She shot him a concerned glance and saw he was smiling. Maybe he was trying to play one of his jokes on her again. *But how could he get those people to line up like that outside?* she thought. She just screwed up her mouth and offered him a mute response.

"Mavis, I can see into the future," the baker cooed with intrigue and mystery. "I predict that within the next few minutes, a truck will park outside the shop, and a cheer will go up from the people."

"You couldn't possibly know that, Mr O'Connell," Mavis snapped, looking at the baker as if he'd gone crazy.

Sarah had heard most of the banter between Mavis and her husband and, suppressing a smile, came into the shop to see the remainder of the show.

Sure enough, a few seconds later, the Hoadley's Chocolates truck pulled up outside, and the crowd cheered the driver as he opened the back doors and loaded up his trolley with scrumptious treats: chocolates and sweets of all types and, best of all, Violet Crumble bars. There was no shortage of people to hold the shop door open, and "Good on you, mate" was chorused by all.

Mavis stood silent, open-mouthed—her face moving rapidly from the baker to the fast-approaching trolley loaded high with confectionary.

"G'day, Bill," said the driver. "Sorry, but that's all I've got for you this trip. Supplies are still short, and you're the last stop on the line."

The baker put Mavis out of her misery.

"Mavis, the people living at the start of the long, winding road leading into town would have spotted the truck first and quickly phoned their friends in town," the baker explained.

"'Get down to O'Connell's as soon as you can: the Hoadley's truck is on the way.' That would have been the message, and you can see for yourself what happened," the baker said with a laugh.

"Oh my God, look at the boxes of Violet Crumbles and chocolates and … everything," Mavis said, bubbling with excitement. "Oh, but Mr O'Connell, Mrs O'Connell—there's not enough to go around," she whispered in anguish, noticing the people had now moved to the shop counter and were beginning to shout their orders.

"All hands on deck," Sarah yelled. "Here's the price list, and remember it's only two items per customer."

A good-natured groan went up from the customers, but they grudgingly accepted it was fair enough.

Sarah, Mavis, and the baker spent the next half hour in a frenzy of opening boxes, handing over chocolates, taking money, and giving change. There was still a queue when Bill boomed out the dreaded announcement:

"Sorry, we're sold out—there's nothing left. Hopefully, we'll get another delivery in a fortnight."

The latecomers left the shop disappointed, but some contented themselves by purchasing oatmeal and honey biscuits.

"Nothing left" was not strictly true. Sarah had surreptitiously squirrelled away four blocks of chocolate and half a dozen Violet Crumbles. "Family comes first," she reasoned. And she'd remembered to look after Mavis with a couple of Violet Crumbles.

Still smiling from the Hoadley's truck excitement, the baker walked to the bakehouse at the back of the shop, taking stock of Sarah's and his decision to move to Korumburra. The lush green pastures, mostly cleared of bushland, supported thriving dairy farms, which in turn provided the butter factory with high-grade milk. Production was booming, and most of it was exported to Britain, still experiencing major shortages after the war. The coal mine operated 24 hours a day, turning out fuel to support unparalleled electricity generation across the state. There was even a soft drinks factory. Korumburra was a vibrant business community, and people had money to spend, and spend it they did.

The family business was going well—far better than the bakery at Buchan they'd thankfully sold for a fair price near the end of the war. They'd made good money at Buchan, but tourism was its mainstay and slow to pick up after the war. In any case, the days of supporting a family by baking bread for a small community were over. Korumburra was full of hungry coal miners and workers at the butter factory. And the business offered confectionary and a small line of groceries as well as bread. He was trying to add more baked goods—cakes and buns—but he wasn't a pastry cook, and that was a problem he had to solve if he wanted to expand.

But leaving Buchan wasn't only about business and better opportunities for the family. The ordeal of the murdered Aboriginals at the hands of a local farmer and his son had taken its toll on the baker. He had become moody and withdrawn, suspicious of people and what they may be hiding. While he could be himself with Sarah and the kids, he was wary of strangers and even old friends like Hodges. The fragility of life forced itself into his thinking every day—that human lives can end so suddenly through the unjust, unthinking actions of ordinary people sat like a lead weight on his heart. The spectral Irish priest, once a welcome adviser, had become an object of fear, even loathing. He resented the intrusion of the priest into his life, and his anger escalated quickly whenever he came to mind. As the family left Buchan to move to Korumburra, the baker quietly whispered, "Good bloody riddance," thankful to be leaving the violence he'd experienced there, and hoping above all else, that he would never see the priest again. But he doubted it, and deep down, he sensed the priest was not finished with him—not by a long stretch.

Sarah poked her head into the bakehouse to tell her husband that his mate, Patrick, was on his way to see him, and the worse for drink. She had been looking out the side window that faced the back of the local hotel, and as usual, there were two or three men chatting while they pissed in the garden. Patrick, ruddy-faced, was walking unsteadily towards the back door of the bakehouse and thankfully didn't join his comrades at the garden.

Why on earth don't they use the toilet inside? she thought to herself, shaking her head. Bill had spoken to the publican about it, but nothing changed, and the smell of urine often floated through the bakery windows after closing time at the pub.

Sarah left just as the back door opened, and Patrick lurched in. He was a huge man, heavily muscled, as might be expected of a miner. As usual, the sleeves of his flannel shirt were rolled up, revealing forearms like strands of thick rope knotted together. Dark in complexion, perhaps from the coal dust that had ingrained itself into his skin, he had a lumbering gait that made him steady himself every few steps. And drink only made it worse.

"Hello der, Bill," he slurred, slumping into a chair. His slight Irish accent was more pronounced after he'd had a few.

"I've gone and done it this time—put all my pay into the Salvos' donation box. Christ knows what I was thinking," he groaned, looking at the floor.

"You've what?" the baker yelled, hardly believing his ears. "Jesus, you've got family to support—you can't give your money away."

"I know, I know, but there're miners off work and doing it hard," he said, trying to justify his actions. "There's been some men injured, and…" but he was cut short by the baker.

"You can't look after everyone, Patrick. Your family comes first," he growled.

The two men looked at one another in silence until the baker spoke.

"I'll go around to the Salvos and explain what's happened to Major Henderson," he said. "He's a reasonable man. I bloody well hope he is."

The baker left Patrick sitting head down in the bakehouse and walked briskly to the Salvation Army temple. Major Henderson was expecting him.

"Mr O'Connell, seems like we've just received a rather large donation," he said, with a bemused expression on his face. "I gather you've come here on behalf of Patrick to relieve me of it."

"That's about the strength of it," the baker replied. "You know what he's like when he's had a few drinks—too generous for his own good."

"Quite so," the major replied, handing the baker a wad of notes. "And talking about his drinking, I'd appreciate you encouraging Patrick to come and see me—we might be able to help him with his problem."

"I'll do what I can," said the baker. "His drinking has become worse lately—he needs help desperately. I'll try to bring him over tomorrow after he's sobered up."

The baker went home and found Patrick much as he'd left him.

"Make sure you give most of it to your wife," he said as he handed him the money.

"Oh, yes… I promised Major Henderson that you'd go and see him tomorrow… about your drinking problem. I'll take you there myself. Agreed?"

"Alright," Patrick muttered hesitantly while getting to his feet. "You're right. It's time I did something about the drink. It's just that things are getting on top of me –what with safety at the mine and all—"

"Go home and get a good sleep," the baker interrupted. "We'll go over and see the Salvos tomorrow afternoon."

Patrick nodded his head and lurched out the door under the watchful eye of the baker, who was making sure he didn't go straight back to the pub.

Why he'd become friends with Patrick Kearney baffled the baker. They had virtually nothing in common—different trades, politics, and churches. Patrick said he was a nonpracticing Catholic and had pretty much given up on the church. But for some reason, they hit it off from the moment Patrick poked his head in the bakery door soon after the family arrived in Korumburra. He wanted to wish the baker good luck with his new business, and they'd got to talking and had a cup of tea together, and that's when it all started. Patrick stopped by most days for a talk, and the baker, usually repelled by drinkers, tolerated and liked Patrick, even during those times when he was hitting the grog hard. He tried to support his friend as best he could, even though Sarah strongly disapproved and thought Patrick to be a bad influence about the place. When the baker considered why he liked and supported Patrick, he was quick to identify his robust, good humour and dedication to hard work. But mostly, it was his compassion—his concern for his fellow man, particularly the coal miners. Patrick was always helping other men with their hard grind in the mine, and if they were injured or sick, he was the first to visit with a food parcel and money. And there was something else the baker picked up immediately at their first meeting—Patrick's Irish accent, slight as it was. Somehow, it resonated with him, and he knew it reminded him of the Irish priest who he'd first encountered in Bruthen.

There was some meaning in him being drawn to Patrick, but it was obscure and yet to reveal itself.

The baker liked Patrick well enough, but the spectral priest was a presence he had come to dislike intensely. He no longer trusted the priest and deeply resented him intruding into his life and the lives of his family members. Disturbing Sarah and the kids with horrible nightmares infuriated the baker most of all. If the priest couldn't spur the baker into action with dreams and visions, he'd target the family until the baker finally started to seriously consider the cryptic messages he was receiving. Time and again, the baker questioned whether there was a priest, insubstantial and ghostly as he was, or whether it was all just a weird creation of his own mind—a dream he was making appear real by believing it to be so. Sure, at Bruthen, the priest appeared to be real and substantial, and they had even shared tea and food together. But the priest inhabited the night; the only time the baker saw him during the day was on the road to the Mount Welcome mine and that was a dark stormy day bordering on night. At Buchan, he had only observed the priest in the shadows, and he was silent—his form indistinct. The one thing that was clear was the pain etched deeply on his face—a sight the baker recalled so vividly that he felt pain and heaviness in his own heart. But, even so, this priest could be the stuff of dreams, and the baker now questioned the priest's existence. He had come to believe his mind was making things real that were not.

Patrick arrived at the bakery next day at about 2 p.m., apologising for his behaviour of the previous day and saying he was ready to knock off the drink or at least give it a good try. The baker had heard it all before but hoped this time Patrick would be true to his word. They walked around to the Salvation Army hall and found Major Henderson, who took them to a small office and closed the door.

The three men sat together quietly, Patrick breathing heavily and staring at the floor. The baker finally broke the silence.

"Patrick assures me he's going to do his best to give it up this time, Major Henderson. He's got a lot on his plate, but the drink isn't helping."

"Never does," the major replied, searching Patrick's face. "But it's not an easy road. Patrick, do you understand what you're letting yourself in for?"

"I do, sir," Patrick said hesitantly. "But I can't keep going on as I am. I'm no use to anyone."

"Don't underestimate yourself, Patrick," the major interjected. "Your family, your workmates, and Mr O'Connell here respect you—I know that for sure."

Patrick looked as if he was about to burst into tears.

"Let's talk it over, you and me, Patrick," said the major. "I'm sure we can give you the support you need to beat the drink."

The baker took this as his cue to leave and, giving Patrick a vigorous pat on the back, walked slowly back to the bakery, hoping above all else that the Salvos might be able to prevent Patrick ending his days drowning at the bottom of a bottle.

———

There's no stopping dreams, that's for sure, the baker thought as he was plonking dough into high tins, ready to go into the oven. He'd always had lucid dreams, particularly in the last hour of sleep. And being a baker working through the night, that meant sometime in the late afternoon. Since moving to Korumburra, he was sleeping soundly, and his dreams were generally about the business—fears it might lose money or he couldn't get supplies. Not particularly pleasant but not frantic and frightening like his dreams in Bruthen and Korumburra. Thankfully, he didn't seem to be having any waking dreams or visions as had occurred previously—paint-streaked Aboriginals and such. He always listened closely when the family gathered for meals—mostly breakfast—for anyone saying they had had a bad dream, but for years, nobody had reported anything too out of the ordinary.

But lately, his morning dreams contained what seemed to be a symbol of some kind—SS. There was nothing frightening in the dreams, just an SS symbol drawn on walls or furniture or hovering in space. The baker was more bemused than concerned about the symbol, and he thought it would pass in time. But it persisted. The baker would give it a moment's thought before forgetting about it and moving on to other more immediate concerns like running his business.

One morning after he had finished the night's baking, he was sitting down to breakfast with the family when Helen screwed up her face at something she was reading in the newspaper.

"It says here that 'Eighteen members of the German SS have been found guilty of involvement in the *final solution*—the Nazi plan to murder all the Jews in Europe,'" she read aloud. "What does SS stand for?"

"Silly Sausage," Ruthie chimed in. "Anyone who reads that stuff in the paper is a 'silly sausage' including you."

"Shut up, you fool," Helen snarled. "Maybe you'll learn to read the newspaper one day, like… in about fifty years."

"All right, that's enough," Sarah chided. "Eat your breakfast, or you'll be late for school. Sarah rose from the table and went to the bathroom.

But the baker quickly turned to Helen, astonished she had mentioned the SS.

"The SS was a special part of the German army. They were violent men, loyal to Hitler," he said in a low voice. "But why did you read that article, Helen?"

"Well, the SS printed in it caught my eye, and it reminded me I dreamt about a big SS scrawled on the front window of the shop," she said.

"When did you dream about the SS?" the baker asked.

"Last night and maybe a few nights ago, I don't remember," Helen said casually as she returned to eating her porridge.

"O'Connell's Silly Sausage shop owned by Miss Helen O'Connell," Ruthie joked.

Helen screwed up her face at Ruthie, indicating such comments were not worthy of a response.

The baker was relieved Sarah didn't hear his discussion with Helen. She would suspect that family members having similar dreams would be like the time in Bruthen when the entire family was haunted by nightmares of the terrifying doctor. But so far, there was nothing terrible in the dreams of the baker or Helen—only the enigmatic SS. And it seemed like Helen had put the subject out of her mind, and even Ruthie had moved on to packing her schoolbooks. Hopefully, the SS would be forgotten, at least for a while.

Sarah marshalled the girls out the door and saw them off to school before helping Mavis in the shop. The baker remained at the table finishing his second cup of tea, but he was tense and his mood was bleak, as if he had returned to the darkness of his father's mine or the cave at Buchan.

So, that bloody Irish priest returns with his signs and riddles, he thought angrily, squeezing his China cup so tightly it began to crack. *Same routine: come into my dreams with some nonsensical symbol and expect me to work out its meaning and take action to sort out some problem. And if I don't figure it out and fix things, then my family cops the disturbing dreams until I do something.*

He stood up from the table and was about to pitch the cracked cup at the wall but restrained himself.

Maybe SS cropping up is just a flash in the pan, he thought in a poor attempt to convince himself that the priest had not returned and that his mind had once again become overactive. He recalled his brother Joe's stoical advice to forget about spirits and the like and focus on the here and now—family and work.

Sound advice that I should be following, he thought as he walked to the bathroom to wash before turning in for what would hopefully be a deep and dreamless sleep. But in his heart, he knew it had started again.

It was dusk, and low dark clouds floating slowly across the western sky masked much of the glow of the setting sun. He was standing in a familiar place—somewhere near the bakery, but he wasn't certain. If he could turn around, he would see the bakery but was unable to move himself—it was like he was being held in the grip of some unseen force. But he could move his eyes, and as he looked to the left, a street sign suddenly appeared—"Egan Lane." *That's not far from the bakery—just a few streets up,* he thought. He looked down and drawn large in vivid white on the black asphalt road were the letters SS. Then awareness returned, and he lolled in that drowsy state between sleep and wakefulness—calm and breathing slowly and deeply. Egan Lane and SS were clear in his mind. If he were to walk outside, he would be able to clearly see them. He was wracked by a jolt that prevented him going back to sleep, and stark consciousness flooded back, and he sat fully awake on the side of the bed. He rubbed his face and eyes and stretched his frame to its fullest extent. Yes, the dreams were back, and the cryptic symbols with them, of course. He put on his slippers and dressing gown for the walk to the toilet.

Two symbols now: SS and Egan Lane, he thought languidly as he shuffled along without much purpose. He tried to put the symbols out of his mind but quickly gave up. He knew he had to determine their meaning and follow them wherever they took him.

"God knows where that might be," he muttered angrily, shaking his head.

———————————

Sarah was working flat out in the kitchen while catching up on all the gossip as she prepared Sunday lunch not only for her own family but for Bill's recently married brother, Cyril, and his wife, Margaret. And Bill's other brother, Joe, and his wife, Joan, had unexpectedly dropped in for a quick visit, not expecting to be invited for lunch, but not making much of an attempt to decline the offer. Sarah had made a big pot of beef and barley broth and cooked a leg of lamb. She only needed to prepare some more vegetables for the extra guests, and there would be enough for everyone. The baker often mused that Sarah must have been at the miracle of the loaves and fishes in the Bible—no matter how many people she had to feed, everyone received ample, and there were always leftovers.

A rowdy and high-spirited lunch with family and kin was just what the baker needed after his disquieting realisation that the priest had somehow returned, in his dreams at least. He had become withdrawn since the dream, and Sarah had asked him if he was feeling alright. He'd replied he was just tired—nothing that a good sleep wouldn't fix. But he made a mental note to behave more attentively with his family and save his ruminations over the symbols for the bakehouse at night.

There were nine people around the table, keeping their elbows tucked in so everyone had room, and Joe, of course, gave his opinion on all manner of subjects—the conditions in Europe after the war, the moves the government was making to establish a car production industry but his particular concern was the Japanese war crime trials.

"They should hang the whole bloody lot of them, including Hirohito," he said contemptuously. "They're animals, and even animals don't kill without necessity, like the Japs did to our soldiers and civilians."

Everyone agreed, but Cyril quickly added, "Hirohito won't be executed. They're letting him stay on as Emperor. Can you believe that?"

"That's the Yanks for you," Joe snarled. "No doubt they've done some deal with him to allow them to profit from Japan. What about justice for our boys and the civilians they butchered?"

After lunch, the baker and his brothers sat out on the back veranda, talking about business and employment conditions in the country and the government's plans to radically increase migration from Europe.

The baker bided his time and, when the talk died down, he turned to Cyril.

"Helen saw an article in the paper the other day about the German SS and asked me about it," he said. "I didn't really know what to tell her and just said they were bad men. Who were they?"

Cyril was the right man to ask. He'd been captured by the Germans during the allied evacuation from Greece and sent to an Italian prisoner-of-war camp. He escaped with some of his mates and headed for the Swiss border, but was again captured by the Germans, and this time sent to a camp deep in Germany.

"Yes, bad men alright," Cyril said slowly and contemptuously. "They didn't run the camp I was in but visited from time to time and took men away—mostly British aircrew. They'd rough them up right there in the camp in front of us, and then they'd be taken away, never to be seen again—not in our camp, at least."

"They were Hitler's elite troops and fanatical Nazis," Joe advised with an air of authority. He had taken a close interest in the workings of the German army, having been pitted against them in the Great War. "You had to be special to join the SS: strong physique and preferably a blond-haired, blue-eyed German with a German ancestry going back many generations.

"And now they're letting the bastards into our country," he scowled. "Apparently, there are some Germans working in the coal mine down the road."

"What? SS men?" Cyril yelled in astonishment. "Surely they wouldn't let them in? Christ, they'll let the Japs in next."

"I don't know for sure they're SS, but one of the truck drivers I know at the mine told me there are Germans there and more on the way," Joe said. "Italians are alright, but it's too early to let Germans in— too many families lost sons to those swine, just like in the first war."

"Amen to that," Cyril affirmed. "I'll tell you what, Bill. Tell Helen to forget about the SS. Believe me, they are best forgotten."

The Sunday lunch ended soon after. Sarah and Bill walked their guests outside to their cars, enjoying a last-minute chat before waving goodbye as they drove off.

"Poached eggs on toast for dinner," Sarah advised. "I've done enough cooking for one day."

"Suits me," Bill said, with his arm around her shoulders as they walked back into the house. "You outdid yourself with lunch today."

But his mind was not on dinner. He was thinking about Germans working at the mine and the SS. And he knew exactly the man to ask about men working at the mine.

Patrick was getting on the baker's nerves, pacing up and down the bakehouse, engaged in a monologue on the lack of proper safety procedures at the mine. He had been raving for about twenty minutes, his Irish accent becoming stronger the more agitated he became.

"Patrick, that's enough. Give it a break, would you?" the baker said at last, exasperated. "Make us a cup of tea—you must need some refreshment after that rant."

"Ah, I'm sorry, Bill," Patrick said. "It's just that the mine management is playing with men's lives, and they don't care a hoot. We miners shouldn't be working in that mine—we should be on strike, but everyone's after more money, and to hell with safety."

Patrick shuffled over to the sink and filled the kettle, then placed it on the hob. The baker could see he was upset and feeling powerless to prevent a possible tragedy, but in his highly excited state, he was alienating people. He was being seen as a crank who'd lost touch with reality.

Patrick calmed down a little with a strong cup of tea in hand and a crust from yesterday's bread to chew on.

"How are you going with the Salvos?" the baker asked, trying to change the subject.

"I haven't taken a drink in two weeks," Patrick said, puffing up proudly. "They're good people, Bill. I feel a lot better off the drink, and I hope to stay that way, too. I could do without all the worry about the mine, though—if anything makes me start drinking again, it'll be that."

"You can only do so much," the baker advised. "Why don't you try to meet with the union officials? Surely, they'll listen to you?"

"The union boys—they're not really experienced miners," Patrick said. "And there's so much pressure on them from the blokes who are making big money from the new bonus payments for producing more coal in a shift. As I've been saying, the faster they go and the more coal they mine, the more methane is released, and the ventilation systems aren't up to removing it quickly enough. We're heading for an explosion, I'm sure of it."

Both men drank their tea in silence. The baker realised the time was right to probe Patrick for the information he was after.

"I hear there are some Germans working at the mine," he asked.

Patrick was glum and didn't bother to look up from his tea as he answered.

"Yes, that's right. There are three, no four, German fellas who started a couple of months ago," he said disinterestedly. "Good workers, too. Why do you ask?"

"My brothers and their families came for lunch last Sunday, and we got to talking about the German army and that SS division they had that killed a lot of innocent people," the baker said. "We wouldn't want any of those blokes in our community."

Patrick's head snapped up at the baker's words, and his face suddenly flushed, much as it did when he was talking about the mine a few minutes ago.

"No, no," he exclaimed defiantly. "Those lads are alright—they wouldn't harm anyone. They're only interested in making a new start, and they get on well with all the blokes. Their English is improving every day—they'll sound like all the other blokes in a few months. What's that you said? SS?"

"The SS was an elite division set up to crush anyone opposed to the Nazis. A mob of them has just been tried for war crimes, and it seems they will go to the gallows," the baker said.

"No, those men at the mine, they wouldn't have been involved in anything like that—was it SS you said?" Patrick responded emphatically. "I've never heard of that before."

"How can you be sure they weren't SS men?" the baker asked before he was quickly cut off by Patrick.

"I tell you, Bill, they're alright, good men," Patrick said, getting agitated. "The mine management, the government—they would check those details. They wouldn't have been allowed to migrate if they'd been involved in war crimes."

"Yes, I suppose you're right. They would have been checked out by the authorities before they came here," the baker agreed. "Anyway, from what you've said, it sounds like we have nothing to worry about."

Patrick resumed his nervous pacing, but he was not talking about mine safety now.

"They're young lads—in their twenties—they deserve a fresh start in a new country," he said bluntly, looking directly at Bill, ensuring he knew he was serious. "I know what it's like to leave a country going through tough times and come to a place where you can start again. Those men should be left in peace. No one should be judging them."

The baker was about to explain that he wasn't accusing the German men of anything, but Patrick, who was becoming increasingly nervous and agitated, went to the bakehouse door to leave.

"Fair's fair, Bill," he said firmly. "Everyone deserves a second chance. And I don't want to hear about that SS or whatever it is again."

The door closed with a thud, and the baker was left to ponder Patrick's reaction to his questions about the German miners.

Fair enough; honest people deserve new opportunities to work and prosper, he thought. But Patrick's defence of the Germans? Somehow, it seemed a bit strong.

What preyed most on the baker's mind was that Patrick had become upset when he first heard the term SS. And the baker was determined to find out why.

The girls had gone to bed early, and Sarah and Bill were having a cup of tea together before the night's baking began. Bill thought Sarah had something on her mind and was trying to find the right time to talk to him. It looked like that time was now.

"Bill, you know, and everybody knows you're a master baker, and your bread is the best anywhere," Sarah said slowly and with great care. "But we must face it—the days of the small country bakehouse are just about finished."

The baker had been expecting Sarah to raise this with him. He'd seen her scanning the newspapers and reading the advertisements about the big baking companies that were taking over the trade in Melbourne.

"Erica Stevens told me the other day that her sister and neighbours in South Melbourne get their bread at the local grocery shop now," Sarah explained. "It's good bread, apparently, freshly baked each day and cheaper than our loaves."

Sarah was trying to speak as caringly as she could because she knew they had to make a decision that would impact the whole family and Bill especially, who stood to lose his trade and the means of providing for his family.

"Some people have said the grocer in Dandenong is stocking bread, and the local bakery is closing," Sarah went on. "Dandenong is what? An hour and a half's drive away. Pretty soon, we'll be seeing bread trucks arriving here like the Hoadley's truck, only every day."

There was silence as they both considered the changes taking place in their country. Australia was following America's example: factories were producing food of all types, and people couldn't get enough of it. And as Sarah said, it was good and cheaper than locally produced food.

"I thought selling stuff like chocolates and canned goods might support the bread trade but, you're right—if our bread sales drop, we don't have a business," the baker said. "I can make a few buns along with the bread, but not enough to make a difference. Pastry cooking—buns, cakes, and pies—that's the way to go, but I'm no pastry cook."

"Why don't you talk to your cousin, Harry, in Melbourne?" Sarah suggested. "He's a good pastry cook, and his shop is doing well. Maybe he could advise you about picking up the skills for pastry cooking—maybe even teach you himself."

"It's been in the back of my mind," the baker said, even though his thinking in recent times had been focussed on the SS and German miners. "You're right to bring it to a head, darling—it's best we make the move into a different business before it's forced on us."

Sarah ambled over to her husband and held him in a huge hug, and kissed his cheek.

"We'll be alright. You learnt to be a good baker, and you'll be a good pastry cook. You'll see," she said soothingly.

"Yes, alright. I've got to start the baking, or there'll be no bread tomorrow," the baker replied, reluctantly removing himself from his wife's embrace. "And I'll call Harry on the phone tomorrow and arrange for both of us to talk with him."

———

Early next morning, Patrick poked his head through the bakehouse door, a strained smile on his face.

"Still talking to me?" he joked, though he looked tired and worried.

"Of course, get yourself in here and sit down," the baker said.

Patrick ambled in, stretching himself before sitting down and watching the baker knock the last of the loaves from the oven out of their tins.

"God, it's a beautiful smell in here," Patrick said. "It's such a lovely, comforting, wholesome aroma—restores your faith in the good of this world. I suppose people have loved the smell of freshly baked bread for thousands of years, do you think?"

"Yes, I suppose you're right," the baker replied. "You're quite the philosopher this morning, eh?

"Aha—me, a philosopher?" Patrick chortled. "I don't think so. It's just that sometimes you realise it's the simple things you'll miss most when you die."

"Yes, like good friends," the baker said. "Patrick, I didn't mean to upset you yesterday asking about the Germans at the mine. And I didn't mean to reflect badly on them. As you say, they're probably good men trying to make a new start."

"Bill, I'm sorry—I overreacted and got myself upset," Patrick was quick to say. "The German lads seem alright, I suppose—I don't really know them very well. The talk about the SS - it confused me. I'm not sure why, but it did."

The tension between the baker and Patrick dissolved, and they again found the warmth they shared in each other's company, even during periods of silence when they were left to their own thoughts.

But the baker had not forgotten about the SS and Patrick's reaction and confusion. He had to find a new approach to discovering what Patrick knew about SS, even if it lay hidden deep in his mind.

"I've known you for about three years or so, Patrick, but you've never told me about why you came to Korumburra or your life before Australia," the baker said, hoping that Patrick might open up about his past and inadvertently reveal something about SS.

"Yes, you're right, Bill—my past is a closed book to just about everyone, but I don't mind telling you," Patrick said amiably, having relaxed considerably since reconciling with his friend.

"I'm not prying—just interested, and whatever you say remains between us," the baker said.

"Right you are, Bill, but I don't have much of the story to tell you," Patrick replied. "As you know, I'm from Ireland—Dublin born and bred. I've lost my accent over the years, and to be honest, I've worked hard to lose it by talking exactly like the local men at the mine. Still, when I'm upset or angry, the old accent returns, as you know. Where should I start my story? Well, I was headstrong and reckless as a young man, but if you saw the conditions we lived in, you'd understand why. My god, it was dog eat dog."

"So, it was the tough conditions?" asked the baker. "You left Dublin to escape the poverty?"

"Yes, that's part of it," Patrick replied slowly, staring vacantly at the floor.

"I've never told anyone about this, Bill, and you must promise to keep it to yourself," Patrick said, looking wide-eyed at the baker. "I know I can trust you."

The baker sat down next to Patrick and assured him his story would go no further, not even to Sarah.

"Times were very tough in Dublin, and then the war started in 1914," Patrick said. "I was seventeen—too young to enlist, and in any case, I had no intention of doing so. I made my money where I could—labouring for a day or two here and there, running errands, and I was a bit light-fingered too. Nothing big and only from those who could afford it. Anyway, Easter 1916 comes along, and the Irish nationalists—they wanted Ireland to be independent from Britain—staged a rebellion. They occupied the General Post Office and other buildings and started shooting at the English troops stationed in the city. It was pandemonium for days: shootings and killings on the streets at all hours, shops being looted. Some of the things I saw would amaze you."

"Like what?" the baker asked.

"Try this for size," Patrick said. "Just down from the post office, I saw a beautiful young woman staring at the new fashion clothes in a shop that had just had its front window broken. Without a word of a lie, Bill—she stripped down to nothing—stark naked—and then dressed herself again with clothes from the shop. That stopped people in their tracks, particularly the men, for a couple of minutes, I can tell you.

"She was completely naked?" the baker interjected, totally astonished.

"As the day she was born," Patrick said. "See, Bill—that's what poverty does. She'd probably been wearing the same cheap, thin clothes most of her life, and there she is in front of an open shop window full of beautiful warm clothes. What would you do? What would any of us do?"

"Grab some clothes and go somewhere private to change," the baker suggested timidly.

"Ha, ha, me too," laughed Patrick. "But that lass wasn't waiting any longer for her new clothes, and she didn't care who was looking.

"Anyway, food was what I wanted—for my family and neighbours—we were nearly starving most of the time in those days," Patrick explained. "So, I went down to Sackville Street, and a grocery store there had had all its windows shattered, and the shelves were full of canned goods and packages of food. A crowd had gathered, and everyone had the same idea, so I bolted through the smashed front window, grabbed a hessian bag from the floor, and started to fill it as quickly as I could. Canned meat, fish, fruit, and small bags of flour—I couldn't think what to get next. With my bag full, I pushed my way through the people who were stripping the shelves bare—they even tried to grab my stuff, but I pushed them away right enough. When I got outside, there's a fella yelling at me to stop stealing and put it all back. He was yelling at everyone coming out of the shop."

"Who was he—the shop owner?" the baker asked. "You couldn't blame him for trying to keep his goods."

"No, not the owner, but a fella I sort of knew," Patrick explained. "Then, I remembered he was a public speaker– a pacifist, anti-war, and for women's rights— I'd heard him speaking on the steps of the Customs House. His name was Skeffy or something. And he came up to me and yelled right into my face:

'I think I know you, so put the goods back and tell the others to do the same. You've no right to steal anything.'

"I laughed, and pushed past him and took the food home," Patrick said. "But then I remembered he'd said he knew me, and I began worrying that he might inform the police. So I went back to the store, hoping I might find him and explain that my family really needed the food. He wasn't there, but a fella told me he was planning to hold a public meeting that night to speak against the looting."

Patrick stopped talking at this point, trying to gather his thoughts, but his breathing had become rapid and shallow.

"Are you alright," the baker asked. "You look a little shaky."

"I'll be alright—just getting my breath," Patrick mumbled in a trembling voice.

"Where was I? Oh, yes, the public meeting," Patrick said. "So, I went to the meeting, and this fella stood up. People called him 'Skeffy' and he wanted everyone there to help him stop the looting that was going on. There weren't many people there, and no one was much interested in what he had to say or helping him. But he spotted me again and said he reckoned he knew me and that I must stop stealing and help him persuade others. I laughed in his face and left the meeting hall, certain now that he was going to turn me in to the police or the British forces who were fighting the rebels. When this Skeffy came out of the hall, a gang of people from my neighbourhood started yelling at him—saying he was against the poor. I followed them, and as we were approaching the Portobello Bridge, I saw my opportunity. British troopers were guarding the bridge, and their officer obviously didn't like the look of the noisy crowd. So, I went up to his sergeant and said to him: 'That fella they're yelling at - he's a Sinn Féiner—you better be careful of him and don't believe a word he tells you.' Next thing I know, the officer has him arrested and taken away, probably to the barracks. And I thought, well, that gets me off the hook—they won't pay any attention to what he says, particularly about me."

Patrick had become agitated and was sitting and then standing as he told his story, trying to relax and draw even breaths but unable to do either. The baker was concerned about his friend - his hands were shaking, and his restless movements increased as each minute passed.

"Patrick, sit down and relax yourself—this story of yours is making you ill," the baker ordered.

But Patrick was on his feet again, pacing around the bakehouse, hands and lips trembling.

"No, no - I must finish my story, Bill, now that I've started," he gasped. "Next day, it was getting on towards night, I ran into a friend of mine, and he tells me the British executed that Skeffy fellow along with two other chaps. Apparently, they thought he was Sinn Féin," my friend said. "God knows why they'd think that—he was a pacifist, you know.

"You could've knocked me down with a feather," Patrick went on. "Christ, I never thought they'd do that. I thought they'd rough him up and jail him for a few months - but execute him? And I was the one who informed on him. I was in a terrible state, knowing I had sent a man to his death. I was in a panic and could hardly walk, but managed to find my way to a church, and sat in the pews trying to recover. Then, this priest approaches me and asks do I need assistance. Straight away, I asked him to hear my confession—I had committed a dreadful sin, the worst. Anyway, he hears my confession, but I didn't even get to finish it before he starts on me.

"'How could you betray that man?' he yelled. 'He was my friend - a man of peace and compassion, and you've given him up to the British who are looking to wipe out the Sinn Féin.'

"I said I knew I'd done a terrible thing, but he became even more angry. Finally, he said I was a Judas, and he didn't want me in this church.

"'Ask forgiveness from God not me,' he yelled, as I left the church.

"I went home and realised I had to leave Dublin quickly. Everyone would be looking for me—the British, Sinn Féin, and even the pacifist friends of Skeffy—all trying to blame me for his death. Next day, with the little money I had, I was on a ferry to Liverpool and joined an Irish unit in the British army under a false name. Then I went to the Western Front as a sapper; digging and repairing trenches. That's where I met up with Australian soldiers, and they told me about the country and work prospects. So, at war's end, I hopped onto a ship and found my way to Melbourne, and ended up in Korumburra."

Patrick was incapable of standing by this time and had collapsed into a chair. The baker brought him a glass of water, but Patrick's hands were shaking so much he couldn't properly get the water into his mouth. His whole body trembled, and his breathing was rapid and raspy. Wild, flashing eyes revealed the terror that had gripped him, and a foul odour arose—obviously his bowels had loosened.

"Patrick—stop there, don't go any further with your story," the baker commanded. "Don't say a word more. Just concentrate on calming yourself down."

Patrick became calmer and more composed over the next few minutes, but he was exhausted and deeply depressed. The baker assisted him up and said he would help him to get home. The two men walked out of the bakehouse—Patrick supported by the baker—and they started up the road towards Patrick's house. But they had only gone a short way when Patrick broke from the baker's hold and stood by himself on his own two feet.

"Bill, I've never told anyone that story, and you must swear to me on all you hold dear that you won't tell a soul about it," Patrick said sharply. "Not a word, Bill!"

"Patrick, I promise not to tell anyone about your story or what just happened," the baker replied firmly. "You know you can trust me."

But Patrick was distant and even suspicious. He still looked stunned and unsteady, and there was a dark patch of perspiration across his brow. He stared with fiery, almost threatening eyes at the baker before breaking off and lurching home without even saying "good day."

The baker walked slowly back to the bakehouse, stunned at what had just happened. He also knew that the pieces of the puzzle he was trying to solve were coming together and beginning to reveal their message, but they were not giving up their secret easily.

———

Sarah and Bill took the train to Melbourne early one Friday morning to visit Bill's cousin, Harry, and discuss learning pastry cooking. They planned to go shopping at the city's department stores before taking the tram to meet Harry at his Mont Albert bakery and then catch the late afternoon train back to Korumburra.

As soon as the train was underway, Sarah started dozing while Bill sat quietly reading the newspaper. But he was not focussed on catching up with the news—he was mulling over recent events and dreams to see what sense he could make of them. He took stock of his findings: he had the SS from his dreams, and Egan Lane had popped up in his dreams, too. What had dawned on him most in recent days was the mystery certainly had something to do with Ireland and past events. The ghostly priest was Irish, Patrick was Irish, and the story Patrick told him the other day occurred in Ireland. And who was Skeffy? How did all of those things fit together? That was the question. He tried to identify some way he could start to untangle the puzzle, but it wasn't readily obvious.

As the train sped towards the city, he recalled the time in Bruthen with the Irish priest, Father Doolan, and realised he never did establish when he'd come to Australia and, if so, to which parish. The priest said he'd been in Dublin and visited a church where the mummified remains of crusaders were interred—St Michan's church, the baker vaguely remembered.

The baker had asked after the priest at St. Mary's Catholic Church in Bairnsdale but to no avail. Then, the ghostly image of the priest had presented itself as he drove away from the church with Joe. Perhaps a starting point might be to establish whether the priest ever arrived in Melbourne and, if so, when? Not a great lead, but worth a try. The baker decided that while Sarah was busy shopping, he would make enquiries at St Patrick's Cathedral—the main Catholic church in Melbourne.

When they reached the city, Sarah checked her shopping list of clothes and the department stores she wanted to visit.

"We've only got a few hours, so I'm going to have to move quickly," she said. "If you're planning to look at menswear, I'll leave you to it."

Bill said he might look for a new pair of trousers at Fletcher Jones in Collins Street, so they agreed to shop separately and meet under the clocks of Flinders Street Station in three hours. She gave him a kiss on the cheek and took off at a brisk pace.

He waited until she was out of sight, then caught the tram to the top end of Collins Street and walked a short distance to St Patrick's Cathedral. He paused out front to admire the magnificent spires and the bluestone church they towered above. *How does it go? Build your faith upon a rock*, he thought. *They certainly did that.*

The interior of the cathedral took his breath away. A deep serenity filled the scented air, and subdued light, filtered through stained-glass windows, accentuated the peace and reverence of this holy place. The baker walked slowly down a side aisle of the church, trying to keep his footfall light so as not to disturb the people scattered around the pews who were praying or marvelling at the wonder of the place they were in.

"Good morning," a voice said warmly, coming from somewhere in front of the baker.

The baker had been lost in his study of the vaulted ceiling and stained-glass depictions of biblical stories. He lowered his eyes, and before him was a young priest smartly dressed in a black suit and obviously intent on talking to him.

"Good morning, Father," the baker whispered. "I was just admiring your beautiful church."

"Beautiful it is," the priest said in a resonant and cheery tone, far louder than a whisper that made the baker jump a little. "First time here?"

"Yes, it is, Father," the baker said. "I am actually here to make enquiries about a priest—an Irish priest - who may have been based here years ago. Name of Father Doolan."

"An Irish priest named Doolan—that narrows it down," the priest joked. "At least it's not Murphy! When was he here?"

"Probably arrived after the Great War—maybe around 1920," the baker replied, screwing up his face with uncertainty.

"Well before my time," the priest said. "I should ask why you want to know about this priest, but I suppose you have your reasons."

The baker sighed, thankful that he didn't have to make up some bogus reason for his enquiry.

"Let's say there are several people interested in Father Doolan," the baker said, keeping his response suitably obscure.

"I can't help you, but I know who can, and I was just on my way to see him," the priest said, thinking out loud. "Would you care to accompany me?"

"Is it far?" the baker asked. "I have to meet my wife at the station in a couple of hours."

"No, it's a ten-minute walk—the retired priests' home in Carlton," the priest said. "Ah, I haven't introduced myself—I'm Father Murphy, Brendan Murphy."

The baker thought the priest was joking about his name, then saw he wasn't.

"Bill O'Connell—I'm a baker - from Korumburra," the baker stammered as they shook hands.

"And a good Catholic with a surname like that," the priest remarked, setting off towards the side exit. The baker smiled as if in agreement, thinking it best to let the priest assume that he was a Catholic.

A short time later, they climbed the steps of a three-storey Victorian terrace house, and the priest rapped the brass knocker on the front door. A slim, middle-aged nun with a scowl on her face opened the door slowly, peering hesitantly around the edge.

"Oh, thank God it's you, Father," she sighed with relief. "He's right off his rocker today—can't get the radio working or something."

"Alright, Sister Agnes—I'll see what I can do," the priest said with a laugh. "Go and make yourself a cup of tea and put your feet up. Oh, this is Mr O'Connell from Korumburra. I brought him to see Father Lanegan."

The nun looked the baker up and down, nodded a polite greeting, and went off towards what must have been the kitchen from the smell of boiled cabbage coming from that direction.

But the stale and musty air of the hallway reeked mostly of urine, and the baker felt a slight heave in his stomach. Two old men wearing thick grey jumpers and black trousers shuffled along a passage towards the sitting room, where another man sat in a padded armchair, staring off into space.

"Fragrant, isn't it?" Father Murphy said as he led the baker up the stairs before knocking on a heavy white door and pushing it open.

"Father Lanegan, are you there?" Father Murphy yelled. "I've brought someone to see you."

"Of course, I'm bloody well here, and there's no need to shout—my hearing is fine," a deep Irish voice yelled.

The door opened with a rush, and a thickset white-haired man—standing at least six feet tall, but slightly stooped, stood glaring at the two visitors. His face was crimson with anger, and small strands of white spit hung from his bottom lip.

"What seems to be the problem, Father?" Father Murphy said in a singsong voice as if speaking to a child.

Father Lanegan sensed the indulgent tone, and his mouth tightened as if he was going to give Father Murphy a piece of his mind, but he had a more urgent issue.

"Bloody radio is fritzed, and the horse racing preview is on," he said angrily. "See if you can fix it—I've tried everything. The bloody valves are probably blown."

"It's Friday today, Father," Father Murphy said. "The horse racing is on tomorrow."

Father Lanegan grunted dismissively as he lowered himself into a lounge chair.

Father Murphy walked over to the radio and tried the switches and dials with no effect. Then he looked at the lower wall behind the radio.

"Simple enough to fix, Father—you have to switch it on at the wall plug," Father Murphy said, trying to suppress a smile.

He bent down and switched on the power, and the radio blared into life at a deafening volume. He quickly turned it down, set it on the right radio station, and switched it off.

"Well, who the bloody hell turned it off at the wall switch?" Father Lanegan roared. "I bet it was Sister Agnes—she's always messing around with things."

"Now, now," Father Murphy chided. "Sister Agnes looks after your every need. She's a great comfort - an angel."

"Bloody fallen angel, if you ask me," Father Lanegan said pointedly. "And who is this fellow you've brought with you?"

"This is Mr O'Connell from Korumburra and he is a baker," said Father Murphy. "He wants to find out about an Irish priest named Father Doolan who came to Melbourne around 1920 or thereabouts. Is that correct, Mr O'Connell?"

The baker nodded, but he was overawed by the sheer presence of Father Lanegan, who now eyed him severely as he lounged back in his seat.

"Father Doolan, eh?" the old priest murmured in surprise. "Yes, I knew a Father Doolan—an Irishman—came here in 1920, the same year as me. We came on the same ship from India. What more can you tell me about the Father Doolan you're interested in?"

The baker's heart jumped when he heard India—that's where Father Doolan said he'd been when he first talked with him in Bruthen.

"He was from Dublin and had visited St Michan's Church, and when he was in India, he spent time in Cochin in the south of India," the baker said slowly, trying to recall the exact details.

"Yes, that's Father Seamus Doolan, all right," the old priest interrupted. "He told you the story about the mummified crusader at St Michan's, did he? I'm from Cork myself—never been to St Michan's, but I've been told by several people it has mummified remains in its crypt. Now, what exactly is your interest in Seamus?"

Both Father Lanegan and Father Murphy turned and looked expectantly at the baker.

The question he had been dreading sounded as if someone had struck a gong. The room was so quiet the baker could hear his own breathing. But he was mute, and no matter how many half-baked reasons for his interest in Father Doolan flashed through his mind, not one sounded convincing enough to put into words.

It was Father Lanegan who broke the silence and the sudden tension that had arisen in the room.

"Father Murphy, you've done me a great service today by fixing my radio and bringing Mr O'Connell to see me," the priest said. "I suggest it would be better if you left us now so we can continue our discussion in private. If I'm not mistaken, there are sensitive matters we need to consider."

"Oh, yes—that's fine, Father," said Father Murphy. "I'm due back at St Pat's in any case. It was good to meet you, Mr O'Connell, and I hope we'll see you again."

Father Murphy nodded his goodbyes and quietly left the room. They heard him in the hallway saying a warm goodbye to Sister Agnes, assuring her that everything was fine.

Father Lanegan and the baker sat in silence, studying one another. The priest had a deep, penetrating gaze as if searching your soul, and the baker averted his eyes several times.

"Let me start out by saying Seamus was an unorthodox man. Some questioned his sanity, including me," the old priest said in a steady voice, looking towards the ceiling. His gaze once again fell on the baker's face, and he shifted in his seat to get closer to him as if he suspected someone might be listening.

"I'll tell you what I know about him and also about our discussions, but you must promise to keep everything confidential," the priest said. "I suspect you've had contact of one type or another with him, and I've no desire to know the exact details, do you understand?"

"You have my word," the baker replied, still astonished that the priest actually knew Father Doolan. His anxiety about what he would be told was almost unbearable.

"Try to relax now," the old priest said, sensing the baker's escalating unease. "I assume you want to learn something specific about Seamus, and I hope I can tell you, but understand that I don't know his whole story.

The baker nodded and moved closer to the old priest, who was now speaking just above a whisper.

"Just after the Great War, the Catholic Archbishop of Melbourne, Daniel Mannix, sent word to the Church in Ireland that he desperately needed priests to minister to his large Irish congregation. I was a priest in Cork, and the opportunity of relocating to Melbourne appealed to me greatly - better climate and all that. Eventually, I was accepted and set off in July 1919 from London. We sailed via Suez and reached Bombay in India, and that's where I fell sick with a fever. I was put ashore in hospital, and the ship sailed on without me. Bombay was where I first met Father Seamus Doolan. He had just returned from Cochin in the south of the country—he'd apparently carried out a study for the

Archbishop of Bombay on allegations of unorthodox practices and teachings among the Cochin parishes. He'd left Ireland in early 1919 and when he arrived in Bombay, he was directed to report on activities in Cochin and delay his journey to Melbourne."

Father Lanegan paused to gather his thoughts and take a sip of water.

"He once told me that the Buddhists and Hindus had the right idea about the nature of the universe, and he'd got to know about their teachings in Cochin," the baker said as Father Lanegan took some deep breaths.

"Precisely, but I didn't understand how much he had accepted such views—unsound as they are—until much later," Father Lanegan remarked contemptuously so as to leave no doubt about his aversion to Father Doolan's views.

"Seamus was one of the kindest men I've ever met," the old priest continued. "He helped nurse me back to health, and in November, we secured our passage to Melbourne, arriving as the congregation was preparing Christmas celebrations. But no celebrations for us—two weeks after arriving, we were both down with the Spanish flu."

"Archbishop Mannix was beside himself. He'd secured two Irish priests for his congregation and was now in danger of losing them to the flu. He had us isolated at St Vincent's Hospital and even brought in a specialist doctor to treat us around the clock. Can't quite remember his name."

"The doctor's name was Crawford," the baker said knowingly, looking the priest straight in the eyes.

"Yes, by God—that's it—Crawford!" Father Lanegan said in amazement. "How did you know that?"

"Long story," said the baker. "I knew there was a connection between Father Doolan and Doctor Crawford but I didn't realise it started then."

"He was a strange man—Crawford—always fussing around Seamus and me, poking injections into us," Father Lanegan said. "I didn't like him or trust him, and as soon as I felt the worst of the flu was behind me, I refused his treatments. But Seamus—he thought the doctor was a saint—a true healer. What became of Crawford, do you know?"

"Killed himself and most of his family in a botched medical experiment in 1925," the baker replied, not hiding his disgust for the doctor.

"Good God—I had no idea," the priest exclaimed. "Where did it happen? In the town of Bruthen?"

"No, in Prahran, just a few suburbs across town," the baker answered. "Why do you mention Bruthen?"

"Seamus—he and I were still good friends then—came to me one day to borrow money," Father Lanegan said. "He told me he had to visit Crawford urgently in Bruthen. Apparently, he'd moved there to open a medical practice."

"What year would that have been?" the baker asked.

"Oh, a few years after we arrived in Melbourne—maybe 1923 or thereabouts—can't remember precisely," the priest said.

1923, when Doctor Crawford killed the Lamberts. He must have contacted Doolan to tell him what he'd done and get his advice on what to do. And they decided, or rather the doctor decided, I bet, to hide the bodies in the Mount Welcome mine.

"Mr O' Connell—are you alright? You seem to have drifted off somewhere," Father Lanegan said in a raised voice.

"Sorry, Father, something just occurred to me, but I'd like to hear the rest of your story," the baker said. "You were saying that Father Doolan and you ceased being friends."

"For two or three years after we arrived in Melbourne, we were like brothers," the priest said. "Of course, I was aware of his unorthodox views, such as his acceptance of reincarnation, but he kept it private. And he was such a hardworking, compassionate priest—visiting the sick and troubled at all hours. But all that changed, and he became belligerent—taking a stand against church doctrines and promoting his views, particularly on the existence of spirits and reincarnation. He soon ran into trouble with the archbishop and senior officials in the church. They said he was confusing people in the congregation, so he was moved to Ballarat, to an administrative position there, and told to keep his views to himself. I lost contact with him, and the only thing I heard was he sometimes visited towns around the state—God knows why. Then, in the late 1920s—1928, yes, it was when Charles Kingsford Smith flew across the Pacific—I was given news of the flight on the same day as I was told Seamus had been found dead one morning—apparently passed peacefully in his sleep. But I've no doubt he died a sad and troubled man as if he had not fulfilled some desire."

"Did he ever mention the initials SS to you?" the baker asked in a low voice.

"SS, did you say? Like the German SS division?" the priest responded with surprise. "Where on earth did you hear that term, and why would Seamus know anything about the SS?"

"I had a vivid dream, and SS was written in large letters across the road in Egan Lane in Korumburra," the baker said firmly, trying to get to the point of his visit. "I think my daughter also dreamt about SS—it means something, and I need to know what that is."

"Oh, I see—we're looking to interpret our dreams, are we—like that Austrian fellow—Freud?" the priest said sarcastically. "We all want to kill our fathers and marry our mothers. Complete rubbish."

"I believe Father Doolan has the power to present symbols and signs in people's dreams - my dreams and those of my family," the baker said tentatively, expecting fierce opposition from Father Lanegan.

And that, indeed, is what the baker received.

"Mr O'Connell, I'd estimated you to be a reasonable man but now you're starting to sound like Father Doolan," the priest said sharply, raising his voice. "That's the kind of poppycock he raved about—cryptic signs, reincarnation and, for all I know, the dead communicating with those still living. I'll have none of it."

"I'm sorry if I have offended you or your faith, Father," the baker said. "Please try to understand me—I don't want to believe in these signs and secret messages in dreams either, but I know they are real. They've helped me several times put to rest the unfinished business of tragedies from the past."

The old priest sat silent for a minute, eying the baker suspiciously, trying to determine if he was the rational man he first thought or shared the same deranged views as Father Doolan.

"I can't accept your view, Mr O'Connell," the priest said dismissively. "You are suggesting that Father Doolan has some form of spiritual being and is able to influence your dreams—is that it?"

"I know it sounds crazy, but he's able to enter my dreams and those of my family," the baker responded, disappointed that the priest was rejecting what he knew to be true. "But he only presents strange symbols—and there is a hidden meaning in them that I must discover to solve the riddle and set me on the right track to putting things right."

Again, the priest remained silent, his eyes fixed on the baker.

"And you're good at interpreting these symbols, are you?" the priest asked.

"It takes time, but eventually, I work them out," the baker responded.

"As I said, I'm not one for interpreting dreams, but if I were, I can see one clue in the dream you told me about that you have failed to recognise," the priest said. "You said you were in Egan Lane. Transpose the words, and you have Lane Egan, and joined together and dropping an 'e,' you have 'Lanegan.' Is that how it works? Your dream was telling you to seek me out."

"That's it, brilliant!" the baker exclaimed. "That's exactly what the dream was telling me, and you've confirmed it. Now, we need to interpret SS and the full meaning will become clear."

The priest stood up from his seat and walked unsteadily towards the window, gazing out over the moss-tinged slate roofs of nearby cottages. The baker sensed the priest was about to bring their meeting to an end and hoped he wouldn't close his mind entirely to finding the meaning of SS.

"Well, I'm not sure I can help you any further, Mr O'Connell," the priest muttered, still looking out the window. "Seamus and I had such bitter disagreements about these unorthodox notions. They ruined our friendship, and that is the tragedy for me—I admired and respected the man immensely before those pernicious views took hold of him."

The priest walked over to the baker, who was now standing by his seat, and they shook hands. The meeting was over. The baker walked towards the door, but as he was about to leave, turned to the priest and looked him directly in the face.

"Father, I know I am asking a lot of you, but I won't be able to solve the meaning behind SS without your help," he said imploringly. "You are right—I was directed to see you in my dream because you hold the key to the mystery. Please try to think of anything that might help me solve the mystery. I believe it means ending the suffering of Father Doolan and God knows how many others."

The priest nodded his understanding, but the baker was uncertain whether the priest would consider his request any further or close his mind to it forever.

———————————

Sarah and Bill's discussion with Harry went much better than expected. Not only was Harry willing to teach Bill pastry cooking, but would employ him as his assistant in his Mont Albert shop. Harry had built up a good business, but recruiting decent pastry cooks or even apprentices was proving difficult. So, when Bill asked about learning the trade from him, Harry readily agreed and saw it as a great opportunity to gain some much-needed help.

"Bill, you'll be an expert pastry cook in no time," Harry said confidently. "Your bread-baking skills are second to none, and they'll stand you in good stead for making cakes and pies—nothing too fancy but that's what people can't get enough of right now."

"It's good of you to offer me a job as well as teach me the trade," Bill said. "We have reasonable savings that might have tided us over while I was learning, but getting a wage—well, that will make it much easier."

Sarah was beaming and bubbling with excitement at Harry's offer, but she was trying to keep it suppressed. She knew Bill had doubts about leaving Gippsland, but the thought of moving the family to the city and all the opportunities it presented for everyone was a dream come true for her. Good jobs in shops for the girls, and they could find husbands with well-paid office jobs. Most of all, the girls would not end up marrying farmers and living tough, lonely lives on the land, taking care of a tribe of children.

Sarah couldn't hold back any longer.

"Harry, this is a wonderful opportunity—I really don't know what to say," she gushed. "Yes, I do—you won't regret your decision because Bill will be the best pastry cook ever under your guidance—you wait and see."

Harry and Bill both laughed out loud.

"Crikey, don't build me up too much," Bill said. "Let's take it a day at a time."

"Oh, go on with you!" Sarah said. "You've been making beautiful buns and cinnamon scrolls as well as bread for years. And they've always sold out."

Their spirits lifted, Sarah and Bill left Harry's place to catch the train back to Korumburra.

Once on the train, the baker's thoughts returned to his discussion with Father Lanegan, but he struggled to make sense of it.

———————

The first batch of loaves were in the oven, and the baker took a break for a cup of tea. In the cold early morning, nothing stirred in town except for the sound of the wind strengthening from the southwest. A sudden howling gust made him look up from the table and brought him back to reality. He had been lost in thought about the mystery of SS and how Father Lanegan seemed to hold the key to the mystery but was not cooperating. He wondered about making another visit to the old priest but knew that Lanegan had closed the door on any further conversation. And Patrick was avoiding him and had taken to the drink again. Apparently, he was making speeches while half drunk in the pub most evenings about the unsafe mine conditions but was being shouted down by other miners, and eventually, he'd leave downhearted after a nod from the publican that everybody had heard enough.

The baker felt as if he'd reached a dead end. Determining the meaning of SS was crucial, but he couldn't find a way to decipher it. He'd tried writing it down and looking at it every which way, but it was impenetrable. Some part of the puzzle was missing.

He finished his tea and slowly returned to preparing the next batch of loaves for the oven. Suddenly, he became aware that the bakery had turned chilly. He checked to see if a window was open as cold air would ruin the proofing of the bread. The windows were shut, and he searched around quickly to find out what was making the temperature fall. Even when he stood by the oven, there was a distinct chill in the air. Over near the proofing racks, in a dim corner of the bakery, a bread tin dropped to the ground with a metallic clang. And then another. Someone or something was moving about.

"Who's there?" the baker barked in a threatening tone. "Show yourself."

But there was no response.

The baker walked closer to the proofing rack and saw two bread tins on the floor covered by shadow. In the corner of the room, a figure was starting to appear - dark and hunched over with just a small white square apparent—a clerical collar. And as if uncoiling itself like some large snake, the head and shoulders of the phantom rose up and turned slowly to face the baker. It was Father Doolan or some ghastly form of him. His face was contorted into a dreadful grimace, and his open mouth was a dark and gaping hole that looked ready to scream out in agony. The eyes pierced the darkness with ferocity and menace, focussed directly on the baker's eyes, and a vile stench of decay wafted from him as if he'd climbed out of a tomb he'd been rotting in for years.

"It's you, Father, is it?" the baker said in a trembling and uncertain tone. He was straining his eyes to make out the details of the figure that was now moving slowly out of the corner and creeping along the back wall.

"Forgive, forgive," the figure seemed to whisper, but the baker was unsure of what it was saying and tried to turn one ear closer.

"Shhh," the figure hissed like a vicious snake that has been cornered.

The baker was backing away from the loathsome figure but steadied himself.

"What are you trying to tell me?" he yelled in frustration. "For Christ's sake, just come out and say it!"

But the phantom was growing dim, and within seconds, it had disappeared through the bakery wall. The baker, standing open mouth in amazement and apprehension, thought for a moment of tackling the figure and wrestling it to the floor, but it was no use; it was gone. And suddenly, warmth returned to the bakery.

The baker collapsed into a chair, aware that he was trembling all over but not from the cold. The phantom was dreadful to behold, reeking of putrid decay and demonic in the way it stared into his very being. And he knew it carried a message—certainly of immense pain and suffering, but more that it had appeared now in a final desperate appeal to him to solve the cryptic message that lay within SS.

The baker felt sick to his core, badly shaken by the appearance of the phantom, and anxiety was tightening its grip on him because he had no idea of the meaning of SS. And while he thought he may have seen the last of Father Doolan as a phantom figure, he knew he could still show up in his dreams—or those of this family. The thought of his family being subjected to nightmares orchestrated by the priest angered and frightened him. He had to find a way—the merest suggestion of a way forward that might lead to the meaning of SS. And the only lead he had right now was Patrick, who had reacted to the mention of SS but had not said why.

The sickly smell of stale beer, infused with equally stale cigarette smoke, filled the baker's nostrils as he paused in the doorway of the hotel's public bar. He glanced around the dreary room, its floral carpet threadbare, and the yellowing walls, lined with faded newspaper clippings of sportsmen and racehorses, permeated by years of tobacco smoke. It made his stomach turn. He spotted Patrick leaning against the bar, a sudsy glass of beer in hand, regaling a group of three men who were looking at him with suspicion and defiance.

"And I'll tell you again, it's not safe," Patrick slobbered, trying to make his point by lifting his beer glass and downing the contents in one draught.

"You're wrong, Patrick—dead wrong," one of the men replied caustically. "You're only jealous you're not making the big money some of the young blokes are. You need to remember—you're past working that hard, and you shouldn't begrudge it to those who can."

"Oh, is that right?" Patrick protested bluntly.

He was about to raise the stakes in the argument, but the men walked away, but not before warning him to keep his mouth shut or he might suffer some unfortunate consequences—from the young blokes.

The men brushed past the baker, leaving Patrick standing alone at the bar, silent and swaying unsteadily. He turned suddenly as if to shout something at the retreating group and suddenly saw the baker.

"Bill, what the hell are you doing here?" he said, amazed and confused. "Christ, you're not taking to the drink, are you?"

"No fear!" said the baker. "But I need to have a word with you—outside of this hole, preferably."

The publican was cleaning glasses and raised his eyebrows at the baker's remarks. But he said nothing and focussed again on his cleaning.

"Sure, sure," Patrick said. "I was just about to leave anyway."

He gave a cursory nod to the publican, who responded in kind, all the time keeping his eyes on the baker.

The two men walked out to the back of the hotel, keeping clear of the garden bed that doubled as a urinal.

"What is it you want?" Patrick asked with amiable curiosity, trying not to slur his words.

"Do you know a Father Lanegan in Melbourne?" the baker asked.

"Lanegan? No—who is he?" Patrick responded. "I don't know any priests in Melbourne, even Korumburra, for that matter. I told you I've given up the church."

"I went to St Patrick's Cathedral in Melbourne to try to find out about an Irish priest I once met and that SS symbol I was asking you about," the baker said. "Luckily, I was introduced to Father Lanegan, and he told me about the priest I once knew."

"Hopefully, he solved your problem with SS," Patrick interjected with a laugh.

"No, unfortunately—he couldn't help there," the baker said. "But as I said, he did tell me about the priest I met years ago—Father Doolan. Have you heard of him?"

"Doolan, did you say?" Patrick muttered with little interest, but then straightened up and faced the baker as if he'd been pricked by a needle. "There're many priests named Doolan, I suppose. But as I say, the church means nothing to me now—glad to be rid of it. I saw too much of it years ago - always criticising the people it's supposed to be helping."

"Patrick, I desperately need your help," the baker pleaded. "Something must have happened years ago in Ireland, and maybe a Father Doolan was involved. And the SS, whatever it means, was part of it. Think hard, man."

"Oh, for Christ's sake, Bill—leave off," Patrick roared, swaying and menacingly making fists with his gnarled hands. You're just going over old ground, and I've no interest in doing that. Is that all you've come to see me about?"

"All right, Patrick, calm down," the baker said defensively, seeing Patrick's fingers were turning white from the tightness of his fists. "I know this might sound strange, but I believe my trying to find the meaning of SS will be of great benefit to you, and maybe you know that."

"I've heard enough, Bill," Patrick yelled angrily. "I don't need your help or anyone else's. And finding out what bloody SS means won't help me in the slightest. It's just some lunatic fantasy you've dreamed up. You're the one who needs help."

The baker stood silent, lost for words. He was frantically trying to think of some way to keep Patrick talking until he perhaps unwittingly said something that revealed the meaning of SS. But Patrick had closed himself to any more questions.

"I've got far more on my mind than your stupid questions, Bill," Patrick said firmly, having calmed down slightly but beginning to walk away from his friend. "It's the conditions at the mine I care about, and I mean to fix that problem once and for all."

Patrick steadied himself and looked at the baker.

"I don't want to see you again, and I don't want you trying to contact me—best we go our separate ways," he said coldly.

Patrick turned his back on the baker and lurched towards the main street, presumably heading home. The baker watched him leave, saddened at losing his friend, yet surer than he'd ever been that finding the meaning of SS was about relieving Patrick's suffering. But he also knew that Patrick would not be the person to help him decipher SS.

The baker sat on the edge of the bed before taking his afternoon nap. He was tired and anxious, thinking he had too much on his mind. Sarah and he had finally decided to move to Melbourne as soon as they could and take up the offer of learning pastry cooking. The money they had saved, along with the weekly wage from Harry and the proceeds from the sale of the business in Korumburra, would tide them over until they could start their own cake shop in Melbourne. The business agent already had several buyers interested in their Korumburra business. It all seemed squared away, but he was still troubled about moving away from Gippsland and whether he could run a successful business in Melbourne. Leaving familiar country for a big unknown city seemed a huge risk, but Sarah's confidence and energy had finally won the day.

SS was as elusive as ever, and the baker was beginning to think he had met his match with this puzzle—he was making no headway whatever and becoming increasingly desperate in his quest for a solution. The other night he'd had a brainstorm and convinced himself SS stood for State School. He'd run up the road to the Korumburra State School, to see what he could find. But after half an hour of fruitless searching around the classrooms and grounds, he realised it was a dead end—another one, like the Germans at the mine. In low spirits, he slowly tramped home.

His friendship with Patrick was well and truly over. Patrick crossed to the other side of the street whenever he walked past the bakery, even averting his eyes and pretending to be interested in the contents of the shop windows opposite. The baker missed the warm good humour of his friend, who now turned an icy shoulder to him, and the distance between them was a chasm that would seemingly never be bridged.

The baker's head flopped onto the pillow. He could feel his insides churning, and his heart pounded then fluttered as if it was unsure of what to do. Amid his worries, the baker slowly drifted off. A spasm would cause him jump occasionally and make him catch his breath, but finally, he settled into a restful sleep.

Egan Lane at dusk lay before him; familiar yet ominous. The air was cool and still, and he was alone. The soft glow of light from nearby houses gave him some reassurance that other people inhabited this stark place. A low rumble came from the distance, but its cause was a mystery. Gradually, a form took shape—a truck moving slowly along the road, jerking up and down from the rough street surface. As it drew level with him, it hit a large pothole and dropped violently before suddenly rising again, as if an explosion had occurred beneath it. Such was the force of the movement that the lettering on the side of the truck "South Spring Dairy" fell off piece by piece onto the road. The baker immediately took it upon himself to restore the sign and began picking up the letters and replacing them on the side of the truck. The truck driver, oddly familiar in profile - a large man - offered no help. He noticed the letters had not fallen off the sign "Egan Lane" but returned to his task. Finally, he finished. "South Spring Diary." He looked closely at the sign— something was wrong, and yet he had the feeling nothing was wrong. After a few seconds, he transposed the 'i' and 'a' but somehow, it felt like he was making a mistake. The truck drove off and disappeared into the darkness.

The baker woke from a deep sleep. His eyes felt as if they were filled with sand, and he blinked and rubbed them repeatedly until the grit was gone. He lay in bed, deeply relaxed, and each breath brought more comfort and reassurance. He pondered his dream—Egan Lane—again. That was Father Lanegan. South Spring—the initials of the mysterious SS. "Dairy" was right, but somehow it wasn't. "Diary" felt right, but it wasn't. Nobody drove a truck named "South Spring Diary" - it had to be "Dairy." And who was that fellow driving the truck? Father Doolan? No, too small. Maybe Father Lanegan—possibly.

He swung his legs out of bed and sat on the edge of the bed, still half asleep. He knew he'd been given crucial clues, but now he had to put them together into something meaningful—something he could act on. He put on his dressing gown and slippers, remaining quiet so as not to let Sarah and the kids know he'd woken. He needed time alone. As his faculties returned, he decided to itemise what he'd learnt from the dream. Firstly, Egan Lane meant Father Lanegan, meaning he would need to visit the priest again. Second, the truck driver—it must be about Lanegan again—pointing to him being in the driver's seat—the one who could direct him to the solution to the mystery. South Spring was obviously referring to SS. Dairy and Diary. He knew it had to be Diary, but whose diary? Finally, he was in Egan Lane at dusk. Perhaps it meant the curtain was rapidly falling on this mystery—solved or unsolved. If it was unsolved, the suffering of Father Doolan and God knows who else would persist with little chance of resolution. The path became clear in the baker's mind: he had to contact Father Lanegan, who could tell him something about a diary that would uncover the meaning of SS.

"Good morning, Sister Agnes speaking," said a high-pitched voice on the telephone.

"Oh, good morning, it's Bill O'Connell here, Sister," the baker said. "You might remember me—I visited Father Lanegan along with Father Murphy a couple of weeks ago? Father Murphy fixed his radio."

"Yes, I remember you, and I must say that Father Lanegan has changed considerably since your visit—he's gone very quiet; brooding over something he won't talk about," the sister said bluntly, in an accusatory tone. "Frankly, I am worried about him—his time among us may be coming to an end."

"I'm sorry to hear that, Sister," the baker said with concern. "He gave me great support—I hope I didn't tire him too much."

"Who knows?" she replied impatiently. "And what is the reason for your call, Mr O'Connell?"

"Sister, I need to see Father Lanegan again and as soon as possible," the baker said, more as a directive than a request. "I need his advice about something."

"Impossible," the sister snapped. "The man is ill and not receiving visitors. As I said, he seems to be entering his final days."

The baker felt he was up against the Great Wall of China, and Sister Agnes was about to block his last chance to solve the mystery. He collected his thoughts as best he could to work out a new angle of attack.

"Sister, I shouldn't tell you this, but during my conversation with Father Lanegan, we touched on deeply personal and disturbing matters from the past. I believe I now have information that might relieve the pain that arose in Father Lanegan at that time. Please, I beg you, I need to see him and acquaint him with what I now know."

There was silence at the end of the line for almost a minute before the hesitant and suspicious voice of Sister Agnes once again resumed.

"No, seeing him is impossible," she said sternly. "He is a hermit in his room, having no contact with anyone other than me. He takes his meals in his room and spends much of the time sleeping. Whatever it is you want to tell him will have to be said to me so I can pass it on. That's the only way."

"I was really hoping to see him again," the baker said with disappointment.

He thought for a moment about what to say next and how he could convince Sister Agnes to relay his cryptic message.

"It's true to say, Sister, that my talk with Father Lanegan ended abruptly, at his request. We had discussed his dear friend, Father Doolan, and raking over the details of the end of their friendship obviously upset him. Despite their differences, I think Father Lanegan kept an open mind on whether his friend's views were plausible. Sister Agnes—I know there is a diary somewhere that will reveal a message to end the suffering of tormented souls. And I believe Father Lanegan knows whose diary it is and where it is located. Would you please ask him to find the diary and help me to discover its message?"

The phone was silent again, and the baker sensed Sister Agnes was weighing up what to do. Finally, a hesitant voice answered.

"Mr O'Connell—your request is very strange indeed," Sister Agnes responded. "I'm not sure what to make of it, but I'll not stand in the way of alleviating suffering, as you say. I'll pass your message on to Father Lanegan and let him decide on the best course of action. That's the best I can do."

The phone call ended, and the baker knew everything was now in the hands of Father Lanegan. He was unsure as to how the priest would respond, but as he paused to recall the character of the man, he sensed the priest would not abandon him.

––––––––––

The baker was on his way back to the bakehouse when he heard Mavis shrieking for him to come back to the shop. He wasn't expecting another delivery of chocolate from Hoadley's or to see a crowd of people outside the shop. But that's exactly what he saw as Sarah joined him to find out what was happening.

"That friend of yours, Patrick the coal miner—he's gone off his rocker, Mr O'Connell," Mavis blustered excitedly. "He was waving his fist in a gentleman's face. Lord, I thought he's going to flatten him."

The baker was out the front door in no time, walking straight into an unruly mob watching two men jostling one another and arguing violently. Patrick had the general manager of the coal mine, Arthur Ferguson, up against a wall and was shaking him by the shirt collar.

"You bloody well listen, and listen good," Patrick roared, his face red with anger. "The ventilation—it's not up to scratch—there's too much gas building up in the mine."

Two heavily muscled young men, obviously miners, stepped in and seized Patrick's arms. They walked him backward and pushed him into the gutter.

"That's enough," one of them yelled. "You leave Mr Ferguson alone—you're a crackpot."

"Crackpot, eh?" Patrick said loudly. "Sonny, take it from someone who knows what he's talking about—that mine is not safe—there'll be a gas explosion at the rate we're cutting out coal."

"Is that right?" the miner replied. "More chance of you exploding from the grog I can smell on you. Go home and sleep it off, you silly old bugger."

The young miners walked over to see how Mr Ferguson was faring. Patrick was unsteady, trying to regain his feet. The baker walked over and took his arm, managing to get him upright before Patrick ripped his arm away and stood away.

"Take your hands off me," he barked. "I don't want your help."

Patrick and the baker stood glaring at one another until Mr Ferguson, flanked by the two young miners, pushed forward and stood before them.

"You are Patrick Kearney, aren't you?" the manager hissed angrily. "Well, Patrick Kearney, you can report to the mine office and collect what's owing to you. You're finished—you can't treat me or anybody else like that and expect to get away with it. I've a good mind to report you to the police."

Patrick looked as if he was about to tackle the manager again, but the young miners quickly stepped in and pushed him down the road.

"Go home and sober up, you drunk," one of them yelled.

Patrick stood motionless for a moment, then lurched off slowly, mumbling to himself—looking very much a pathetic and beaten man.

Mr Ferguson, still flustered from his encounter with Patrick, walked off briskly, accompanied by the young miners. He was telling them in no uncertain terms that he knew how to deal with the likes of Patrick. The crowd gradually dispersed, and the baker went back to his shop, occasionally looking to see if Patrick was getting home safely.

"He's hitting the drink harder than ever, isn't he?" Sarah said as the baker came in the front door.

"Yes, he certainly is," the baker responded. "I'm not trying to make excuses, but his worry about mine safety has got on top of him. He's not thinking straight, and he won't accept help from me or anyone else. Christ knows what he'll do next."

"Bill, you need to be careful of him—he could end up hurting you along with himself," Sarah said, rubbing her husband's shoulders.

"Yes, you may be right," the baker said vacantly.

Three days had passed since the baker spoke on the phone to Sister Agnes. He had been pacing around the bakery impatiently, his expectations rising every time the phone rang, only to be disappointed to hear it wasn't for him or it was a supplier wanting an order.

One morning, Mavis poked her head into the bakery to say there was a woman on the phone wanting to speak to him—a Sister Agnes.

His heart skipped a beat as he walked briskly to the shop and cupped his hand around the phone so he wouldn't be overheard.

"Hello, Sister. Bill O'Connell here," he said in a hushed tone. "What news do you have for me?"

"Ah, Mr O'Connell. I've plenty of news, and I need you to listen closely. It's all come to a head here, I can tell you," Sister Agnes said excitedly. "Father Lanegan is in a fit of rage—he's just thrown a book at me and told me to call you."

"I'm sorry to hear that, but perhaps you should start at the beginning," the baker suggested.

"Yes, yes—I'll go back to the beginning," she said, sounding increasingly flustered.

"After we spoke the other day, I had a talk with Father Lanegan," the sister said. "Fortunately, he was in a good mood and prepared to listen to me. I told him about our conversation and said you believed there was a diary that might throw light on the problem you'd been discussing. Mention of a diary piqued his interest and got him thinking. He recalled that when Father Doolan passed away in Ballarat, he left a small case of papers he'd written with instructions that it be forwarded to him. It was sent to Father Lanegan, but he never opened it, and when he moved here to the old priests' home he brought it with him and stored it in the basement."

"Have you found the case and opened it?" the baker asked, unable to contain his curiosity.

"We have indeed—this very morning," the sister said. "And what papers they are. Writings about reincarnation and spirits—highly unorthodox from the few I read. But Father Lanegan was only interested in a set of books tied together with red tape—diaries written by Father Doolan, dating from the early 1900s and right up to the time of his death. Father Lanegan leafed through them but suddenly stopped in the middle of one that covered 1914–1918—the war years. His whole demeanour changed—he became angry and nervous and even started talking to himself. First, he told me to put everything back into the case and have it burnt. Then he said not to do that, and he paced around this room like a man possessed. Then he picked up the diary he'd been looking at and, looking like he was going to explode, threw it at me, instructing me to phone you and tell you about the existence of the diary and that you'd know what to do with it. Finally, he yelled at me to leave him alone and that I should tell you he never wants to hear from you again."

"Do you have the diary with you, Sister?" the baker said.

"Yes, of course. It's right here on the table."

"Would you be kind enough to look through it—" the baker said before being cut off by Sister Agnes.

"No, no—I want nothing more to do with it," she said abruptly. "I believe Father Lanegan wants you to have it, so it's best I arrange for its delivery to you. "But I will not lay eyes on it again—it's an evil book."

"Sister, it's important that I get that diary as soon as possible, do you understand?" the baker said. "Would it be possible for you to send it by railway parcel service? Tonight's service will get it here sometime tomorrow morning. I'll send you a money order for the postage in a day or two."

"Very well," she replied. "I have business in the city later today, so I'll lodge it at the parcel service marked 'Urgent.' No need to cover the postage—it will be a blessing to be rid of it. And Mr O'Connell, I believe that concludes your business with Father Lanegan and myself. I insist that you refrain from contacting us."

The buzzing coming from the phone indicated the sister had hung up. The baker replaced his receiver, concerned that his access to Father Lanegan had been closed off. Now, it all relied on the contents of the diary and his ability to discern its message to bring an end to the mystery.

The next morning, the baker waited near where the guard's van stopped at the station, hoping to get his hands on the diary as soon as it arrived. Even so, he had to wait for the station staff to sort and register the mail, but within a few minutes, he had signed for the package and was on his way back to the bakehouse to study it.

The diary was a small, thick booklet with a crimson cover bearing a bold handwritten title "1914–1918." The pages were plain, unlined paper, and the writing was compact but easily legible. The baker studied the first few pages—church business, mostly—mass times and scripture readings. He flicked through the pages and came to an entry dated 10 September 1914.

"IRB yesterday decided on armed resistance—what I feared most. God help us avoid violence."

The baker had read about the Irish Republican Army or the IRA, as it was termed in the newspapers, but not the IRB.

Perhaps another Irish political group, he thought.

As he slowly read the next pages—meetings about pacifism and home rule—the baker became aware that he was not alone. He put the book down and scanned every inch of the bakehouse, but there was nothing to be seen. Yet he could feel a presence—the air was charged like before a massive thunderstorm, and his hair bristled. A chill had fallen on the room, and shadows flickered in dark corners.

The baker returned his attention to the diary, knowing full well that he was experiencing the presence of Father Doolan. He held no fear of the priest now; indeed, he welcomed the spectral visitor who might give a sign to help him solve the riddle of SS.

He decided to check what the priest had written about the start of the Great War and went back to entries in early August. One dated 5 August 1914 stated:

"Britain is at war and will drag Ireland into the fight. Now is our time for peaceful resistance—not one drop of Irish blood should fall. We must push for immediate peace."

The baker looked up from the diary, trying to make sense of what he was reading. The priest was clearly a patriotic Irishman, not fond of Britain but against the violence of war and rebellion in his own country.

He returned to reading the diary, and it was then that he saw the entry:

"SS sentenced to prison—campaigning against recruitment. A dreadful indictment on the British for imprisoning a man of peace."

It was the first time SS had appeared in anything other than his dreams. The baker started flicking through the diary at a faster pace, and SS appeared regularly, but there was no indication of the person's full name.

The entries in the diary from mid-1915 railed against the war and the increasing militancy of Irish associations set up to oppose the British. When SS appeared, it was always associated with denouncing violence, either in the war in Europe or against the British in the fight for home rule. SS and Father Doolan were promoting pacifism above all else, even for causes they strongly supported, such as home rule.

The baker was becoming perplexed. He knew SS was a person and that he was a pacifist, but even if he learnt the identity of this person, how would it help solve the mystery? There was something missing—a person or an incident that would reveal the circumstances of some tragedy that had taken place and provide him with the understanding to redress it.

The baker calmed himself and tried to focus his mind on SS—who it was and what it might mean. But his mind was a blank about SS, and he couldn't stop his thoughts recalling the incident outside the shop between Patrick and the mine manager. And a feeling arose within him with great certainty that this mystery was more about Patrick and Father Doolan than SS.

He recalled the time in the bakehouse when Patrick had told him about leaving Dublin. How could he forget it? Patrick had become a nervous wreck, and it was the start of their friendship souring.

What was the event he mentioned—the rebellion in Dublin in 1916? the baker thought, trying to recall the conversation. *And he said it was Easter.*

He went to the centre pages of the book and checked the dates, finding an entry for 10 March 1916. Again, it referred to a pacifist meeting that had been organised by SS and the disappointing attendance. The baker turned the pages carefully, thinking he must be getting closer to Easter. He came to a section in April 1916 where two pages were stuck together, and he carefully unpeeled them, making sure they came away intact. They contained a long entry for Wednesday, 26 April:

"This night, a man came to confess his sins and seek forgiveness. He confessed that he'd informed the British that SS was a Sinn Féiner and that SS was arrested and then executed by the British early this morning. I was shocked hearing SS was dead and had been betrayed by an Irishman. I turned the man out without absolving him and, indeed, cursed him for his actions. Later, I realised my dreadful error and lack of compassion, and my failing mocked and overwhelmed me—it proved that I am the most unworthy of priests."

Everything became clear for the baker. Patrick had been the man seeking forgiveness for actions in betraying SS to the British, and it was to Father Doolan he had gone to confess and seek forgiveness. But Father Doolan was a close friend of SS, and his personal feelings had taken precedence over his role as a confessor—a priest who could offer forgiveness and comfort to those who had sinned. Patrick knew he had not been absolved of his treachery and sought refuge by leaving Ireland, joining the British Army, and then migrating to Australia.

The baker looked up from the diary and, in his heart, tried to imagine the suffering both Father Doolan and Patrick had experienced since that night in Dublin. A priest who had betrayed his vows and a simple man who could not find forgiveness for the betrayal of a fellow man. Their suffering must have been immense, and had almost certainly increased as the years passed.

As the baker opened the diary to resume reading, a small folded piece of paper fell out of the back cover onto the table. It was a yellowed and brittle newspaper cutting, and the baker carefully opened it. It was a short letter to the editor of *The Guardian* by a Mr E.T. Ellis. The date 12 May 1916 had been handwritten in black ink at the top of the article—clearly Father Doolan's writing. The article was headed "Mr. Sheehy Skeffington" but again, in Father Doolan's writing, a name had been inserted above Mr. Sheehy Skeffington—"Francis." The final piece of the puzzle had revealed itself—SS was Francis Sheehy Skeffington. SS had been an abbreviation referring to the surname - Sheehy Skeffington.

Who was this man? the baker thought. He slowly read the article, discovering that Sheehy Skeffington was "a pacifist in every sense of the word" and that "he took no part in the violence of the rising and probably did his utmost to check it."

That's the man Patrick informed the British about—he was the one trying to stop the looting, he thought, as he recalled the details of Patrick's story in the bakehouse. *And a good friend of Father Doolan.*

The baker returned to reading the entries in the diary after 26 April. Father Doolan noted several times in underlined script that he had committed a grievous sin as a priest by abandoning Patrick in his hour of need. However, he didn't refer to Patrick by name, and the baker realised the priest didn't know Patrick. But an entry dated 5 May 2016 referred to a discussion he'd had with a man named Liam O'Flannery, who was present on the night Sheehy Skeffington was arrested. O'Flannery was convinced that one of the leaders of the mob who'd been harassing Sheehy Skeffington near the Portobello Bridge had denounced him to the British. He named the man as Patrick Kearney. The priest made enquiries and found out where Patrick's family lived, but when he went there, Patrick's sister said he had left Dublin without telling anyone where he was going. He may have gone to England because someone spotted him near the Liverpool ferry, but no one was sure of his whereabouts. In any case, Father Doolan noted that the sister seemed to distrust him and perhaps was not telling him the whole story.

The baker skimmed the entries in the diary coming to 5 June 1916:

"Court-martial of Capt. Bowen-Colthurst for murder of SS tomorrow—Richmond Barracks. Belated justice, I pray, for SS."

And on 12 June 1916:

"Capt. Bowen-Colthurst found guilty of murdering SS but insane. God forgive us our weaknesses and violence towards others."

The baker paused to consider what he'd just read. Patrick might have informed on Sheehy Skeffington, but he didn't murder him—that was down to Captain Bowen-Colthurst. And the British court martial had found him insane. Patrick could not have known the man he gave up to the British would fall into the hands of a madman. Still, it was a bad business—Sheehy Skeffington, a good man, murdered, and Father Doolan and Patrick left drowning in a sea of guilt and self-recriminations over their actions in the affair.

The baker continued to read the diary, but references to SS ceased. The priest occasionally mentioned visiting Patrick's family for information but came away empty-handed and with a warning to cease his visits.

It seemed the story had finally played out, but the baker examined the last pages of the diary dated November – December 1918. On 12 November, there was an entry, underlined and in capital letters:

"<u>ARMISTICE ANNOUNCED, 11 A.M. YESTERDAY. PRAISE GOD, THE SLAUGHTER IS OVER.</u>"

Then, the baker saw an entry in mid-December:

"Finally, Patrick Kearney's whereabouts known. Cousin told me he wrote home for Xmas. He is in Liverpool but planning to migrate to

Victoria in Australia to become a miner. And that is where I shall go, and by the will of God, find him and personally grant absolution of his sins."

The baker knew he now had enough understanding to put an end to this tragedy—to the suffering of Father Doolan and Patrick. Patrick needed to know that the man he informed on was not a Mr Skeffy but Francis Sheehy Skeffington, a man of peace, who was wrongly executed. But his death was not Patrick's fault, rather that of a deranged British officer who had been court-martialled and convicted of the murder. Sheehy Skeffington had been a close friend of Father Doolan, the priest Patrick had sought out to confess his false accusation, which went some way to explaining why Father Doolan reacted to Patrick as he did. Patrick needed to know he had been absolved of his sin of denouncing Sheehy Skeffington years ago. And he had to understand that Father Doolan deeply regretted his own sin of abandoning Patrick without forgiveness that night in Dublin in 1916. Father Doolan had written, above all else, that he earnestly sought the forgiveness of God and of Patrick for his failure as a priest.

It was a lot to take in—a tragic tale sparked by false words over three decades earlier. Closing the diary, the baker stood up from the table, wondering how he might get Patrick to listen to him long enough to find out the truth of what really happened and to receive news that he had been forgiven.

All was still in the bakehouse, and the warmth had returned.

The spirit of Father Doolan has departed for God knows where, the baker thought. *He's left the bakehouse, that's for certain, but he hasn't gone far, I'll wager.*

The baker's thoughts were interrupted when Sarah suddenly appeared in the bakehouse out of breath and desperately trying to talk.

"There's pandemonium at the coal mine," she yelled, gasping for air. "Your friend, Patrick, has taken over the mine and ordered everyone out. He's armed with a gun and explosives and says he's going to blow up the place."

"How long ago did you hear this?" the baker asked anxiously.

"Just now—Mavis told me," Sarah said, recovering her breath. "There's a big crowd near the mine entrance. Mavis said they haven't a clue what to do—they're just standing there, talking among themselves."

The baker was quick to react and, grabbing the diary from the table, walked quickly to the front door of the shop.

"Bill, don't you go there," Sarah screamed, running to grab his arm. "Patrick is insane—he could do anything; he'll probably blow himself up."

"Hey, it's alright," said the baker, trying to comfort his wife. "I just want to see if there's a chance I can talk to him. I might be able to talk him out of whatever he's planning to do."

The baker freed himself from Sarah's grip and kissed her on the cheek.

"Patrick would never hurt me," the baker said. "And right now, I am about the only person he trusts enough to talk to."

Sarah released him and watched as he broke into a run and headed to the mine.

The baker went through the main gate and found the scene as Mavis had described. Miners were milling about, talking excitedly, but no one was trying to take control to manage the situation. The baker saw that a barrier had been erected at the mouth of the mine to prevent anyone from entering. He quickly walked over to it and spotted an old miner he knew as a customer at the bakery.

"Jack—what the hell's going on?" the baker asked impatiently.

"Bill—what are you doing here?" the old miner asked. "Best get back—that mad bugger could do anything—he'll bring the whole mine down on himself and us if we don't stand well back."

"Tell me how all this happened—is it about the safety of the mine?" the baker asked hurriedly.

"Yes, yes—the safety of the mine," Jack said. "He makes a good point, but this is not the way to handle it. He turned up here half an hour or so ago and started waving the gun around and ordered everyone out of the mine. After it was cleared, he showed us the explosives and said nobody was to enter the mine, not if they valued their life. He said he wanted the mine manager to turn up and admit the mine is not safe. And then, he ran into the mine, and we heard him operate the lift to go down to the pit face. The manager hasn't showed yet."

"Jack, you have to let me into the mine and take me down the lift to talk with Patrick," the baker implored. "I know I can talk sense to him. You know he listens to me probably more than any other man in Korumburra. Take me in, Jack—for the good of all."

"You're taking a hell of a risk, Bill," Jack said slowly, shaking his head. "If he detonates those explosives, we'll both be goners."

"Then tell me how to operate the lift," the baker said quickly. "I'm prepared to take the risk because I've got information Patrick desperately needs, and it might bring him out with no harm done."

Jack studied the baker closely while rubbing his hand across his dry lips.

"Alright, here's what we'll do," Jack instructed. "Just you and me - we'll go inside, and I'll operate the lift to get you down to Patrick. Then you need to talk fast, mind you, to convince him to give up. I'll only wait near the lift for a few minutes."

The baker and Jack crossed over the makeshift barrier amid the gasps of the crowd and shouts for them to come back. Jack turned to the crowd.

"Bill and me, we are going in to see if Bill can talk sense to Patrick," he boomed with authority. "If that mine manager shows up, tell him to come to the lift and be prepared to talk to Patrick."

The baker and Jack walked briskly into the mine. Jack donned a helmet, and threw one to the baker and told him to put it on. The darkness of the dimly lit mine soon obscured them for the crowd outside. The two men pushed along the shiny black tunnel to the sound of dripping water and their soggy footfalls. The baker felt a shudder in his stomach—this was a hellish place, dank and crumbling—it felt as if the roof might give way at any second. Finally, they arrived at the lift and Jack held the cage door open and directed the baker to get in.

"This here is the switch for the bell," said Jack. "When you want to come up, give it a good hard push and let it ring for a while, understand?"

The baker nodded, and suddenly, the lift dropped down a couple of feet before moving at a steadier pace. In the dark confines of the cage, with little light, the baker could feel his muscles tightening and breathing becoming shallow. The lift seemed to be taking forever to get to the bottom, and the slow drone of the motor echoed ominously around the shaft.

With a shudder and a loud jolt, the lift reached the bottom and stopped. The baker opened the cage door and looked right and left in the narrow shaft, hoping to see Patrick. He saw a dim light on the right side about fifty yards away and slowly edged his way towards it, all the time trying to relax his taut muscles and scratchy breathing and quell the escalating anxiety that was starting to grip him viscerally, threatening to make him faint.

The baker squinted his eyes and finally made out the form of Patrick, sitting on the shaft floor with his back against a wall of coal. He looked to be in a world of his own and was oblivious to the approach of the baker.

"Patrick, is that you, man?" the baker yelled as the echo of his own voice surprised him.

Patrick jumped from his sitting position to his feet in one quick, deft movement when he heard the familiar voice of his friend.

"Bill, is that you?" he shrieked as he looked up the shaft. "I heard the lift and thought the mine manager had finally found the courage to confront me. What in the name of God are you doing here?"

The baker summed up the situation and thought he would try to get the upper hand to get Patrick under control.

"I'm not someone who abandons his friends, Patrick," the baker said calmly, feeling his anxiety subside a little. "Listen, in my hand is a book—a diary. It shines a new light on those terrible events in Dublin years ago that you told me about."

"What are you talking about, Bill?" Patrick said, mystified by the baker's words, still shocked to see him.

"Hear me out, Patrick—you owe me that at least," the baker interjected, determined to make his friend listen to the whole story.

Patrick was about to order Bill out of the mine immediately but held back, intrigued at what he might tell him.

"The story starts on 25 April 1916 when you falsely informed the British that Francis Sheehy Skeffington was a member of Sinn Féin, which led to him being arrested," the baker said, with the knowing tone of someone who understands the whole affair. That's right, his name was not 'Skeffy'—that was probably a nickname—but Francis Sheehy Skeffington, a pacifist and writer. He's the SS I was asking you about—it wasn't the Germans at the mine, but Sheehy Skeffington."

Patrick sat back on his haunches, open-mouthed, eager to hear the rest of the story.

"Remember, you found out the British had killed Sheehy Skeffington, as we now know him?" the baker asked. "And you were mortified because you didn't think they'd do that. So, you went to a church to confess your misdeed and seek forgiveness; only the priest turned on you and, instead of forgiving you, sent you away with accusations of treachery ringing in your ears."

"Yes, that's it exactly," moaned Patrick, his face starting to contort with anguish at reliving the incident again.

"The priest you asked to forgive you was a personal friend of Sheehy Skeffington, and that's why he turned on you," the baker said.

"How do you know this, Bill?" Patrick exclaimed, dumbfounded at the story he was hearing.

"The priest you visited was Father Seamus Doolan, and the book I'm holding in my hand is his diary," the baker explained. "It records the details of the night you asked him to forgive your sin, and it says he refused because of his admiration for Sheehy Skeffington. But listen well, Patrick, the diary also describes the bitter torment Father Doolan experienced at not offering you forgiveness and absolution: his failure as a priest, in his words. And he made extraordinary efforts to overcome that failure and even crossed the world in hope of finding you to let you know that he had forgiven and absolved you all those years ago."

Silence came over the mine apart from the dripping of water from the ceiling and upper walls. Patrick let himself drop onto his backside on the wet floor and still gazed fixedly but uncomprehendingly at the baker.

"I just don't understand how you could come into possession of all those details and that diary—it's impossible," Patrick said, slowly shaking his head in disbelief. "Bill, can you explain that to me?"

"You need to believe me, Patrick, and believe in me," the baker said. "Everything I have told you is the truth. Do you want to read the diary—

the part where you went to the church to confess your betrayal that night?"

The baker held out the diary and took a step towards Patrick, but he was quick to his feet and held his hands up.

"No further, Bill," Patrick commanded quickly, raising his gun slightly. "Take a few steps backwards."

The baker lowered his hand holding the diary and, hearing the threatening tone in Patrick's voice, walked back a yard or two.

"It's no use showing me the diary—I'm lousy at reading," Patrick said. "I don't doubt what you say, but how did you find out all this information and get your hands on the diary?"

"I'm not sure I can answer that question," the baker said with a deep sigh. "I get signs and dreams, and then I'm left to find out what they mean. The SS I mentioned to you came to me in a dream—and it persisted until I found out its meaning. I don't expect you to understand—frankly, I don't really understand it myself but let's accept that I've found out the truth of what happened between Father Doolan and you."

Patrick stared at the baker wide-eyed, and the expression of doubt on his face betrayed his difficulty in believing what he was hearing. His gaze fell to floor, and his body seemed to collapse as if a huge weight was finally becoming unbearable.

"It's not that easy, Bill," Patrick snarled. "As soon as you mentioned SS in the bakehouse that night, I knew who you were talking about— Sheehy Skeffington. I've tried to forget his name for years, but it won't go away. I committed a terrible act of betrayal against that man. No, I'll carry the guilt with me to the grave."

"There is forgiveness, Patrick—you must understand that," the baker quickly responded. "Father Doolan forgave you and prayed for you many times. And you didn't kill Sheehy Skeffington—it was a British officer who ordered his death, and he was convicted of the killing at a court martial and found to be insane."

"But I was the one who informed on him—a false accusation," Patrick countered. "I should have known what the British would do to him—they were brutal, do you understand?"

"The fact remains—the British officer was the murderer, and that was proved at a British court martial," the baker said forcefully. "You are taking responsibility for a crime that was not of your doing—it's wrong."

Patrick stood silent, wanting to rebut the baker's argument that diminished his guilt, but the information about the court-martialled British officer surprised him and challenged his insistence that Sheehy Skeffington's death was solely his responsibility. Suddenly, a noise like a shovel falling to the mine floor resonated through the shaft.

"Who the hell is there?" Patrick yelled, jumping to his feet and peering angrily towards the lift. "Who did you bring with you, Bill?"

"No one—I came alone!" the baker protested.

But he started to feel a chill in the air and sensed the presence of something, or maybe someone familiar.

Again, the metallic sound came from down the shaft and echoed against the walls.

"There's someone down there," Patrick barked. "Come out and show yourself."

But there was only silence as the two men stood peering into the distant darkness. Patrick swung his eyes onto the baker and realised he knew who was there.

"Who is it, Bill? Come on, out with it," Patrick demanded.

The baker knew that explaining the presence of a man who had died years ago would be nigh on impossible. But he suddenly hit upon an idea—a long shot—that might convince Patrick.

"In the diary, Father Doolan found out you'd departed for Australia from your cousin," the baker said. "But the diary doesn't mention your cousin's name, and I have no way of knowing what it is. Is that correct?

"It is," Patrick said cautiously, wondering where the baker was going with his question.

The baker turned around and saw a metal toolbox with a smooth top about three yards away.

"Let's check the top of that toolbox and see what it reveals," the baker said. "Just trust me."

After a moment's hesitation, the two men walked slowly to the box and Patrick's mouth dropped open, and his face whitened as he saw letters traced in the dust.

"Leo—is that it?" the baker said, reading the script out loud, relieved and astonished his gamble had paid off.

"It's a trick of some kind," Patrick bellowed. "His name is Leo, alright, but how the hell did that writing get there? Who wrote it?"

A sudden gust of air came from nowhere and erased the letters drawn in the dust.

"See that? It's Father Doolan and he is here with us—in spirit, at least," the baker said quietly and assuredly.

Patrick was stunned by the baker's words, but he had to accept them. He rapidly looked around the shaft, trying to identify a figure or sign that would confirm the baker's advice. After a minute or so, he walked back down the shaft, but a peace had descended on him - his face and body were relaxed, and his breathing deep and regular. A soft glow even radiated from this face.

"So many years of suffering for Father Doolan and myself, and God knows how many others," Patrick reflected. "And in this hell hole, he finally brings me the forgiveness I sought all those years ago. So be it."

The baker looked closely at Patrick and saw a man with a great burden lifted. A tear trickled down Patrick's cheek, which he quickly wiped away, but there was no mistaking he was at peace with himself—a peace that had eluded him for many years.

"That's an end to it, Bill—and now it's time for you to leave," Patrick said with quiet authority. "Off to the lift with you, and get the mine manager to come and talk to me."

"Come on, Patrick," the baker pleaded. "It's over—come back to the surface with me, and you can talk to the manager there."

Patrick took up his gun once more and waved it towards the lift.

"Be off with you, Bill—you've been a true friend to me, and you've brought the gift of forgiveness," Patrick said. "But my work is not done, and I'll not allow any man to die down here through neglect of safety. You get the mine manager to speak to me now, that's all I want of you."

"What can I say to reason with you—".

"It's the mine manager I want now, Bill," Patrick said emphatically, standing erect with the gun cradled over his forearm. "God bless you but go now. And can you take Father Doolan with you, or does he stay here with me?"

The baker knew that Patrick would not budge, so he nodded his head to him in understanding and friendship and turned to walk back to the lift.

"Father Doolan will be with you to the end, Patrick," the baker said assuredly as he set off.

"Tell the manager he's got ten minutes to make contact with me, or else I'll detonate the charges and bring the whole bloody mine down," Patrick yelled to the baker as he entered the lift.

The baker pressed the bell, and the lift jerked unsteadily upwards. He momentarily caught a glimpse of Patrick, standing strong, a serene smile on his lips.

"Well, is Patrick coming out?" Jack said as he opened the cage door for the baker.

"Not yet. He wants to see the manager," the baker said quickly. "Where can I find him? Is he outside?"

"Not sure," Jack replied. "Run out and see for yourself—I'm too bloody slow these days."

The baker ran like he'd never run before and soon found himself in glaring daylight just outside of the mine's mouth. A group of men clustered around him, firing off questions about Patrick and what he intended to do.

The baker searched the faces of the crowd, then saw the manager standing with his supervisors, some ten yards away.

"Patrick wants to talk directly with you, Arthur," the baker yelled as he ran over to the group.

"What's that?" the manager said desperately in a high-pitched voice. "I'm not going to speak to a raving lunatic who's threatening to blow up the mine. He'll take me with him if he can. He's threatened me before, you know."

"He only wants to talk to you about the safety in the mine," the baker interjected. "If you want, I'll go along too—he won't do anything if I'm there."

"No, out of the question," the manager exclaimed, looking to his supervisors for agreement and reassurance. "I won't let a madman dictate terms to me. If you want to go back down the mine, that's your affair, but don't expect me to go with you."

The supervisors dutifully nodded their heads at the manager's refusal to enter the mine, and one of them murmured that Patrick was only trying to lure him to his death. The mine manager's features were becoming paler by the second, and his legs were shaking.

"You are the only one who can talk Patrick out of this," the baker said before the manager interrupted.

"I won't negotiate with that lunatic—that's final!" he said with a tremor in his voice. "I believe he wants to kill me."

The baker turned his back on the group, desperately trying to think of some way to lure Patrick back to the surface. He saw Jack had finally made his way out of the mine and ran over to talk to him and the group of miners who'd greeted him.

"Jack, the manager won't go down the mine to talk with Patrick," the baker yelled. "We have to do something and be quick about it. When I left Patrick, he said he'd blow the charges in ten minutes—time is almost up."

"Nothing can be done, Bill," Jack said, shaking his head. "We could get the manager to the lift in a few minutes, but he won't go, so that's an end to it."

The baker stood there in silence, his mind racing to find some way to stop Patrick from destroying himself.

"The only thing that can be done now is to get everyone away from the mine entrance," Jack said loudly. "The ventilation system down there is not working right—I noticed it when I was waiting at the lift. If there's gas in the mine, Patrick's charges will make for one hell of an explosion. Come on! Everyone needs to move well back."

The people assembled near the mine began to move away, slowly at first, but as the danger posed by a large blast sank in, they started running to get to safety. The baker was reluctant to leave at first, but Jack took him by the arms and frogmarched him towards the gates.

It started as a distant rumble but quickly became a deafening thunderclap that shook the ground under their feet and spewed dark clouds of coal dust out of the mine entrance. The booming echoed from the surrounding hills, and earth tremors were felt underfoot for a minute or more. The emergency sirens wailed, and red danger lights flashed starkly—the whole scene becoming grey from the settling dust. When the noise finally ceased, people turned to look at the mine entrance and saw it had collapsed and was now filled with rock and coal debris.

Dusting himself off, Jack turned to the baker, his eyebrows raised and a knowing expression on his face.

"There was gas in the mine, alright—and a lot of it," he yelled. "A couple of charges wouldn't make that big of an explosion."

The baker sought out the mine manager in the crowd and saw him cowering behind a brick shed.

"Did you hear that, Arthur?" the baker screamed loudly. "Gas! Dangerous levels of gas in the mine. And you wouldn't listen! Patrick had to give his life to prove it, you bloody murderer."

The mine manager quickly composed himself and saw that the miners and even his supervisors were looking at him angrily and muttering accusations that he'd nearly killed all of them through his negligence. A few men started walking towards him, fists clenched, with menacing intentions. The manager sized up the situation and, in an instant, he was in the safety of his car.

"This needs to be reported to the authorities immediately," he yelled as he started to drive off. "The area needs to be evacuated immediately, and I'll see the police attend to it. Don't jump to conclusions—we don't know if gas was the problem—that's a question for the Mines Department."

He accelerated the vehicle and soon disappeared over the crest of a hill, heading into town.

Silence hung like a shroud over the scene, and some of the miners started examining the entrance, assessing what it would take to move the rubble and get down to the pit face. Maybe there was some trace of Patrick to be found, and that could be given a proper burial.

The baker stood near the gate, numb and overcome with grief for his lost friend. The mystery of Father Doolan and Patrick had played out to its tragic end. They had found forgiveness, each for the other, and in doing so, perhaps found the most valuable gift of all.

———

It took a month to remove enough debris to safely recover Patrick's remains. The inquest made a finding of "death by misadventure," and when it was announced, booing and jeering erupted in the court from the miners in attendance. The coroner had stopped short of calling it suicide, admitting the possibility of detonating two charges in the mine might not have resulted in death had it not been for the presence of a high level of explosive gas. The Mines Department was about to open a formal investigation, and everyone knew their inspectors were focussing on inadequate ventilation and gas control issues. Mine management was cooperating, but some supervision staff had already resigned.

The funeral had been well-attended: miners, unionists, and drinking mates mostly. The officiating priest, who hadn't even met Patrick, had to check his notes to remind himself of the departed's name during the brief ceremony. It had been organised by Patrick's wife, estranged from her husband—the result of his many years of alcohol abuse.

The mourners shuffled out of the cemetery, trailing the priest as they headed to the Railway Hotel, where a wake had been arranged.

When they had gone, the gravediggers moved in to finish the job—the dull thuds of the shovelled dirt reverberating on the top of the coffin.

Silence returned to the desolate cemetery on the edge of town as dark shadows lengthened in the late afternoon. The sun was setting behind the steep slopes of a ridge to the west, providing a gentle warmth, but the evening chill was already setting in. The baker sat alone on a stone seat, pulling his coat closed to fend off the cool air descending on him. He was surrounded by those who had once lived but were now entombed in cold ground. He wondered what lives they had led—perhaps they'd lived hard lives, trying to make a living, raising big families, and doing their best to support friends and neighbours. No matter how they lived, they all ended up here—their deeds, good and bad, buried with them—and as the years passed relentlessly, they would be forgotten forever.

Death is the fairest judge of all, the baker thought. *Everyone, rich and poor, wise and foolish, saint and sinner, eventually receives exactly the same sentence—death.*

But is death the end? Are we swallowed for eternity into a meaningless oblivion, never to feel the warmth of the sun, savour the aroma of freshly baked bread, or hear a child's laughter as it plays in the bath?

Father Seamus Doolan learnt in India all those years ago that some part of us persists beyond death, and the baker in his own heart believed it too. But are we fated to return to another life, time and time again, or do we reach a place where ultimate meaning is revealed—heaven? The baker shrugged with uncertainty—it was beyond his understanding.

Yet he knew for certain that the natural process of moving on after death can be disrupted when our deepest spiritual needs are thwarted. When the forgiveness we seek is withheld, or our earthly body is wrongly interred in some wretched place away from one's sacred ground—our migration to another life or realisation can cease until the impediment is removed.

At the behest of the little Irish priest, how many people, now dead, had he helped to move on? Doctor Crawford, the Lambert brothers, the Aboriginal family, and George Davis and his son. Finally, Patrick and Father Doolan himself. Perhaps they would find peace in their journey ahead, but at least they'd been spared the torment of remaining constrained and unfulfilled in some tortuous in-between world.

The last warm rays of the sun were gone, and the eerie hoot of a boobook owl softly broke the silence of the descending dusk. The baker stood from his seat, pausing to look one last time at Patrick's grave. He ambled slowly to the main gate, knowing he had completed his work in Gippsland. The challenge of being successful in an unforgiving city awaited him and his family—away from their own homeland.

Afterword

Francis Sheehy Skeffington a.k.a Skeffy (1878–1916) was an Irish writer, pacifist, and feminist. He opposed the use of violence to achieve political outcomes, and at the outbreak of the Easter Rising in Dublin in 1916, actively took a stand against the looting that broke out.

On the evening of 25 April 1916, followed by a crowd of hecklers he had urged to refrain from looting, Sheehy Skeffington was arrested by British troops near the Portobello Road bridge, wrongly suspected of being involved with the Irish nationalist insurgents.

Later that night, Sheehy Skeffington was used as a hostage by a British raiding party and witnessed several murders carried out by the troops. On the morning of 26th April, Captain Bowen-Colthurst of the Royal Irish Rifles ordered a firing squad to execute Sheehy Skeffington along with two other men.

In June 1916, Bowen-Colthurst was court-martialled for ordering the execution. He was found guilty but insane at the time he issued the order.

Bowen-Colthurst was admitted to the Broadmoor Asylum for the Criminally Insane in July 1916. He was released under supervision in 1918 and, in 1919, migrated to Canada, where he died in 1965.

There is a plaque dedicated to Francis Sheehy Skeffington on the gates of Cathal Brugha Barracks, where he was executed in 1916.

About the Author

Peter Donelly was born in 1952 in Melbourne and attended the University of Melbourne, graduating with a Bachelor of Arts in History and English, followed by a Master of Arts in Public Policy. He was employed for thirty-two years in the Victorian public sector, including eighteen years at Victoria Police.

The inspiration for *The Baker of Gippsland* stems from Peter's parents, who often took the family on holidays to Gippsland and visited towns where they had owned bakeries. Gathered around the card table on long summer evenings, Peter's parents, uncles, and aunts - all captivating storytellers - shared tales of the characters and events that would later shape his writing.

Now retired in inner-city Melbourne, Peter enjoys musing over Buddhist and philosophical works, along with some favourite supernatural classics. He enjoys leisurely walks each day around his beautiful suburb, overseas travel and catching up with his son, daughter-in-law, and two grandsons.

www.ingramcontent.com/pod-product-compliance
Lightning Source LLC
Chambersburg PA
CBHW070358200726

48294CB00003B/968